My Secret Unicorn

A Touch of Magic
and
Snowy Dreams

Two exciting adventures in the
My Secret Unicorn series
together in one bumper book!

*

Have you ever longed for a pony? Lauren
Foster has. When her family moves to the
country, her wish finally comes true. And
Lauren's pony turns out to be even more
special than she had ever dreamed.

My Secret Unicorn

A Touch of Magic
and
Snowy Dreams

Linda Chapman

Illustrated by Ann Kronheimer

PUFFIN

PUFFIN BOOKS

Published by the Penguin Group
Penguin Books Ltd, 80 Strand, London WC2R ORL, England
Penguin Group (USA) Inc., 375 Hudson Street, New York, New York 10014, USA
Penguin Group (Canada), 90 Eglinton Avenue East, Suite 700, Toronto, Ontario, Canada M4P 2Y3
(a division of Pearson Penguin Canada Inc.)
Penguin Ireland, 25 St Stephen's Green, Dublin 2, Ireland (a division of Penguin Books Ltd)
Penguin Group (Australia), 250 Camberwell Road, Camberwell, Victoria 3124, Australia
(a division of Pearson Australia Group Pty Ltd)
Penguin Books India Pvt Ltd, 11 Community Centre, Panchsheel Park,
New Delhi – 110 017, India
Penguin Group (NZ), 67 Apollo Drive, Rosedale, North Shore 0632, New Zealand
(a division of Pearson New Zealand Ltd)
Penguin Books (South Africa) (Pty) Ltd, 24 Sturdee Avenue, Rosebank, Johannesburg 2196, South Africa

Penguin Books Ltd, Registered Offices: 80 Strand, London WC2R ORL, England

puffinbooks.com

My Secret Unicorn: A Touch of Magic first published 2005
My Secret Unicorn: Snowy Dreams first published 2005
First published in one volume 2007
1

Text copyright © Working Partners Ltd, 2005
Illustrations copyright © Ann Kronheimer, 2005
All rights reserved

The moral right of the author and illustrator has been asserted

Set in 14.25/21.25pt Bembo
Made and printed in England by Clays Ltd, St Ives plc

British Library Cataloguing in Publication Data
A CIP catalogue record for this book is available from the British Library

ISBN: 978-0-141-32299-5

My Secret Unicorn

A Touch of Magic

'*All animals can talk. People
just need to listen.*'
Animals couldn't talk. Well, apart
from Twilight, and that was only
because he was a unicorn.
'I just don't get it,' Lauren said as she
groomed Twilight . . . 'What did
Mrs Fontana mean?'

To Holly and Charlotte Allison

Three strides, two strides, one stride . . .
Twilight soared through the air and landed safely on the other side of the jump.

'Good boy!' Lauren Foster exclaimed, patting his neck. Mel and Jessica, Lauren's two best friends clapped from where they were sitting on their ponies, Shadow and Sandy. The three girls had spent an hour after school putting up a course of jumps in the field at Mel's farm.

'It's like he's flying!' Mel called.

Lauren bit back a grin. If only Mel knew her secret! Even though Twilight looked like an ordinary pony most of the time, when Lauren said some magic words, he turned into a snow-white unicorn who actually *could* fly. The only people who knew the truth were an old lady called Mrs Fontana and Lauren's friend Michael, who lived in the city and had a secret unicorn pony of his own.

Lauren pointed Twilight towards the final fence. Mel had decided to put a row of flowerpots in front, which made it look enormous.

Lauren gulped. Suddenly she wasn't so sure about jumping it. *What if Twilight fell . . .?*

Twilight slowed down.

Lauren clicked her tongue, but Twilight got slower still. He was going to refuse! Lauren forced down her fear. 'Come on, Twilight!' she cried, pressing him on. Twilight sped up again and they flew over it.

'Good boy!' Lauren gasped as they landed safely.

'That was great,' Mel said as Lauren trotted over.

'I didn't think I was going to make the last fence,' Lauren replied. 'Twilight slowed down a lot.'

Mel frowned. 'That's not like Twilight. He hasn't hurt himself, has he?'

Lauren felt a flicker of alarm. 'I don't know.' Dismounting, she checked Twilight's legs. There were no obvious cuts or grazes. She picked up his hooves, but they were clear of stones. 'He seems all right.'

'Maybe it was just the jump that made him slow down,' Jessica suggested. 'It *is* really big.'

'Yeah,' Lauren agreed. 'Those flower pots make it look huge.' She noticed that the sun had started to set beyond the mountains that rose up in the distance. 'I'd better go. Are we going to meet up tomorrow and do our school project?'

'Definitely,' said Mel. 'We've still got loads to do. We've got to make our project the best!'

For the last few days, their class at
school had been working in groups.
They'd had to choose a hobby to talk
about and the following week they were
going to present their talks to the class.
Lauren, Mel and Jessica had naturally
decided to do their project on ponies.

'I wish Jade's and David's groups
weren't doing horse riding as well,' Jessica
sighed.

Mel nodded. 'The people who aren't
into ponies are going to get really bored
listening to three talks about the same
thing.'

'We'll just have to think of some way
to make our project different,' Lauren
said. 'We can do that tomorrow.' She

squeezed Twilight on. 'See you guys in the morning.'

As Lauren rode Twilight up the drive that linked Mel's farm with the road, the last few rays of the sun glowed on Twilight's mane. 'You were great today,' Lauren told him. Then she remembered how he had slowed down at the last jump. 'You are OK though, aren't you? You're not hurt?'

Twilight snorted.

Lauren wondered what a snort meant. She knew Twilight understood every word she said, but he could only talk back

to her when he was a unicorn. She felt
slightly alarmed. Maybe there *was*
something wrong and he was trying to
tell her!

They reached the end of the drive.
Lauren normally turned right towards
Granger's Farm, where she lived with her
mum, dad and younger brother, Max. But
now she hesitated. There was a wooded
area on the other side of the road. If she
rode into the trees she could turn
Twilight into a unicorn and ask him if
there was anything wrong.

She checked the road. It was empty.
'Come on, Twilight,' she whispered. 'I'm
going to turn you into a unicorn.'

They entered the trees. Once they were

hidden from sight, Lauren jumped off
Twilight's back and said the magic words
of the Turning Spell:

> 'Twilight Star, Twilight Star
> Twinkling high above so far.
> Shining light, shining bright,
> Will you grant my wish tonight?
> Let my little horse forlorn
> Be at last a unicorn!'

There was a bright purple flash and
suddenly Twilight was no longer a scruffy
grey pony. Instead he had transformed
into a beautiful unicorn with a snowy
coat and a gleaming silver horn in the
centre of his forehead.

'Twilight!' Lauren exclaimed, hugging him.

Twilight tossed his silvery mane. 'Hi, Lauren.' His mouth didn't move but as long as Lauren was either touching him or holding a hair from his mane she could hear him speaking as clearly as if he was another human being.

'Are you OK?' Lauren asked anxiously. 'Why did you slow down at that last fence?'

'It felt like you didn't really want to jump it,' Twilight replied. 'As we were going towards it, you pulled on the reins and stopped pressing me on. I didn't want to jump if you were frightened.'

Lauren remembered the way her stomach had somersaulted when she had turned into the fence. 'I guess I was scared for a few seconds,' she admitted. 'I'm sorry I pulled on your mouth.'

'That's OK,' Twilight replied, rubbing his ears against her while being careful not to catch her with his horn. 'You didn't pull hard.'

Lauren gave him a hug. She was very relieved to find out that he wasn't hurt. 'I'd better turn you back now,' she told him. 'Mum and Dad will be wondering where I am. But I'll come to your field later and we can go flying.'

She said the words of the Undoing Spell and Twilight turned back into a pony.

Lauren mounted and rode out of the trees. As Twilight's hooves clip-clopped along the quiet road, she thought how lucky she was to be able to talk to him. It meant she could always find out if there was anything wrong. She felt her heart swell with love. She had a secret unicorn of her own! Oh yes, she was very lucky indeed.

CHAPTER

Two

'You've been riding late,' said Lauren's dad as Lauren walked into the kitchen a little while later.

'Mel, Jessica and I were jumping,' Lauren explained, sitting down to pull off her boots. Buddy, Max's dog, trotted over to say hello. He was a young Bernese mountain dog and almost as big as a small Shetland pony. He plonked his heavy head in her lap and Lauren stroked him. 'Where's Mum?' she asked.

'Working in her study,' her dad replied. 'I said I'd fix supper tonight.'

Lauren's mum was a writer and she often shut herself in her study for hours at a time when she was trying to finish a book.

Mr Foster stirred some pasta into a pan of boiling water on the stove. 'So, it's Saturday tomorrow. What're you up to? Are you seeing Mel and Jessica?'

'Yes,' Lauren replied, scratching Buddy's ears. 'We're doing a project together on our favourite hobby. We've got to give a talk in front of the whole class.' She frowned. 'I just hope it's interesting enough, Dad. Two other groups are doing their projects on horses too.'

'I'm sure you'll think of something to make your project stand out,' Mr Foster said comfortingly.

'I hope so,' Lauren sighed.

Buddy wriggled around so he was sitting on her feet. He pressed against Lauren's legs, his tail thumping. Lauren laughed. 'Buddy's being affectionate tonight.'

'I don't think Max has fed him yet.' Mr Foster went to the kitchen door. 'Max, come and feed Buddy please!'

'In a minute!' Lauren heard her six-year-old brother call back from the living room.

'Now,' Mr Foster insisted.

'What's Max doing?' Lauren asked.

'Watching some DVD about skateboarding,' Mr Foster replied. 'Steven and Leo lent it to him.'

Lauren nodded. Ever since Steven and Leo Vance had moved into a house just along the road, Max had been really into skateboarding. Leo and Steven who were eight and ten years old, both had skateboards and Max had been going round to play with them at the weekends and after school.

Max came into the kitchen looking grumpy. 'It was just at a really good bit, Dad.'

Mr Foster shrugged. 'Sorry, Max, but

Buddy needs feeding. DVDs can wait.
Animals can't.'

Max sighed but fetched Buddy's bowl.
With his curly brown hair and brown
eyes he looked just like a smaller version
of their dad.

'Is it a good DVD?' Lauren asked him.

Max's eyes lit up. 'It's great! It shows

you how to do all these jumps. Leo and
Steven can do loads of them and I'm
going to learn too. I did a proper Ollie
today!'

'Oh . . . that's good,' Lauren said, not
having a clue what an Ollie was.

'I'm going over to their house
tomorrow to practise some more.' Max
put Buddy's bowl of food down.

'Maybe you should invite Leo and
Steven over here, Max,' Mr Foster
suggested. 'You always seem to be going
to their house.'

'That's because they've got a proper
place to skate,' Max replied. 'They've got
a launch ramp *and* a quarter pipe to
practise on.'

'Well, we could make something here,'
Mr Foster said. 'You could use that
concreted area near Twilight's field – the
place where the old barn was. I could
construct you a ramp or two.'

Max looked at him in delight. 'Really?'

Mr Foster nodded. 'I'll see what I can
do. However, I don't want to see you
forgetting Buddy's supper again, Max.
Having a pet is a big responsibility. You
have to think of his needs before your
own.'

'I'll feed Buddy on time from now on,
I promise,' Max said happily. He stroked
Buddy. 'Sorry, boy.' Buddy looked up
from licking his bowl clean and wagged
his tail.

Mr Foster smiled. 'OK, you can go and watch some more of your DVD. But only ten minutes and then it's supper time.'

Max ran out of the room. Lauren watched him go. She couldn't understand his new craze for skateboarding. It seemed to be all he was interested in at the moment.

Buddy came over and she stroked him. Her dad was right. Since Max had started skateboarding he hadn't been spending nearly as much time with Buddy as he used to. Lauren could feel tangles in the thick white fur around Buddy's collar. When had Max last brushed him? She wasn't sure. Bending down, she kissed the overgrown puppy. She hoped Max was going to start paying him some more attention soon.

That night, when her parents had gone to bed, Lauren crept out to Twilight's field. He was waiting by the gate.

Lauren wasted no time. She whispered the words of the Turning Spell and

Twilight became a unicorn once again.

'Sorry I'm late,' Lauren said. 'Mum and Dad stayed up later than usual.' She scrambled on to Twilight's warm back. 'Let's go flying!'

Twilight whinnied in delight and plunged into the sky. They flew up and up. Lauren's long fair hair blew back from her face but she felt wrapped in warmth. Twilight's magic meant she never felt cold when they were flying – and she never felt tired afterwards. Twilight could do all kinds of magic – special magic to help other people or animals in danger. He could heal wounds, make people feel brave, cut a path through snow and see things that were happening far away. He

had other powers too – powers that he
and Lauren were still finding out about.

Suddenly Twilight slowed down.
'Listen, Lauren! Can you hear that noise?
It sounds like an animal in trouble.'

Listening hard, Lauren heard it too. A
panicked squeaking noise was coming
from the ground beneath them. 'Quick!'
she said. 'Let's go and see what it is!'

Three

Twilight landed in a clearing.

'The noise is coming from over there,' he said, pointing with his horn to a tangle of prickly hawthorn at the edge of the clearing.

Jumping off Twilight's back, Lauren went to investigate. 'Look, Twilight!'

It was very dark but Lauren could see a baby squirrel was caught in the depths of the thicket. Its thick bushy tail was tangled up in thorns and it was struggling desperately.

'Poor little thing!' Lauren exclaimed. She flung herself down on her tummy and pushed her arm through the thorny branches. The squirrel's black eyes darted around frantically.

'It's OK. I'm here to help you,' Lauren soothed. 'Ow!' she cried as the thorns raked down her arm.

'Here, let me help,' Twilight offered. He bent down and started to push the bushes aside with his horn.

There was a vivid purple flash and a cloud of smoke. Lauren gasped and Twilight snorted in surprise. Even the

squirrel stopped squeaking for a moment
and stared.

The long branches had started to
unwind from each other as if they had
come alive.

'The brambles, Twilight!' cried Lauren.
'They're untangling! It must be another
of your magic powers!' she breathed.

Soon, the brambles had untangled

completely and there was a clear pathway
to the squirrel. Lauren edged closer.
Hoping it wouldn't turn round and bite
her, she gently released its tail from the
prickly bramble.

It was free! Lauren wriggled back. The
squirrel looked round at its tail and
suddenly seemed to realize it was no
longer trapped. It scampered out into the
clearing and up a nearby tree. With a
joyful flick of its tail, it vanished into the
leaves.

Lauren smiled. 'It's going to be OK,'
she said, putting her arm over Twilight's
neck and giving him a hug. 'I'm glad we
could help.'

'Me too,' he agreed.

Taking hold of his mane, Lauren swung herself on to his back. A glow of happiness spread inside her. Using Twilight's magic to help animals or people always felt great! 'Come on. Let's fly some more,' she said.

'OK,' Twilight replied eagerly.

Holding fast to his mane, Lauren laughed out loud as he plunged into the sky.

When Lauren woke up the next morning she didn't feel tired at all. She jumped out of bed and pulled on her clothes. She had the whole weekend in front of her!

'We're going to have fun this morning, Twilight,' she said happily as she brushed him after breakfast. 'When I've finished grooming you, we'll go to Mel's house and go riding and then you can go out in the field with Shadow and Sandy while Mel, Jess and I do our project.'

Twilight snorted.

Lauren heard the sound of Max giggling and looked round. He was dragging a large plank of wood across the concrete area next to Twilight's field. Buddy was gambolling around him, getting in his way.

'Get off, Buddy!' Max said, sounding half-exasperated, half-amused.

Lauren went over to the fence. 'What are you doing?'

'Setting up some stuff to make skateboard ramps. Dad's going to come out in a minute and help me.'

'Do you want a hand?'

'Yes, please,' Max replied.

Lauren climbed the fence and took one end of the heavy plank. Buddy bounded around in excitement, almost tripping Max over.

'Buddy! Stop it!' Max exclaimed.

As he lowered his end of the plank, Buddy banged into his legs. Max lost his grip and dropped the plank on his toe. 'Ow!' he cried, hopping up and down.

'Are you OK?' Lauren asked.

'Yeah,' her brother replied, rubbing his toe. 'Dumb dog!' Buddy whined.

'Buddy's not dumb. He was just trying to play,' Lauren protested. She looked at

the confused dog. Buddy wasn't normally
quite so wild. 'Have you taken him out
for a walk this morning?'

Max looked down, his cheeks turning
pink.

'Max?' Lauren questioned. 'You *have*
taken him for his morning walk, haven't
you?'

'Well . . . no,' Max admitted. 'I've been designing my new skateboard course since I got up. I haven't had time.'

'Max, you can't not walk him!' Lauren exclaimed. 'No wonder he's acting so crazy.'

'I'll do it later,' Max said. He went over to Buddy and took hold of his collar. 'Come on, Buddy. You can go in the house. You're just getting in the way.'

'Max . . .' Lauren started to protest.

Just then their dad came walking up to the gate. 'Hi, you two!' Seeing Max pulling Buddy by the collar, he frowned. 'What are you doing, Max?'

'Putting Buddy inside,' Max answered.

'I guess it'll be easier if he's out of

our way,' Mr Foster agreed.

Lauren wondered what she should do.
Her dad didn't know Buddy hadn't been
walked that day. She didn't want to get
her brother into trouble but he was being
really unfair. 'Max,' she hissed. 'Buddy
needs to have some exercise!'

Max ignored her and marched on.

'What time are you going to Mel's?'
her dad called.

'Um . . . I said I'd be there at nine
thirty,' Lauren said, turning to him.

'You'd better get a move on then,' Mr
Foster pointed out.

Lauren headed across the field towards
Twilight. 'Oh, Twilight, I don't know
what to do,' she said when she reached

him. 'I feel really sorry for Buddy but I don't want to tell Dad because then he'll be mad with Max.'

Twilight nudged at his empty feed bucket with his nose. Then he looked at her with his intelligent dark eyes.

Lauren frowned. 'Your bucket? Food?' Suddenly she worked out what he was trying to say. 'You mean I could give Buddy some food? That's a great idea! I could stuff some treats in his rubber toy. That should keep him busy. Thanks, Twilight!'

Twilight tossed his head and Lauren gave him a hug, thinking for the thousandth time how great it was to have a unicorn!

Four

Getting the toy ready for Buddy made Lauren late but she didn't care. She felt much happier knowing that Buddy had something to do while he waited for Max.

Mel and Jessica were saddled up, waiting for her.

'Let's go for a ride in the fields,' Mel suggested.

The three girls rode down the farm track. The sun was shining and the ponies snorted eagerly, pulling at their bits. Patting Twilight's smooth neck, and looking at Sandy and Shadow's pricked ears, Lauren felt a wave of happiness. It was wonderful to be out riding with her friends on such a lovely spring morning. She couldn't think of anything she would rather be doing, apart from flying, of course!

When they got back from their ride, Lauren, Mel and Jessica untacked the ponies and turned them out.

'Where's Samantha this weekend?' Lauren asked Jessica.

Samantha was Jessica's step-sister and they shared Sandy.

'She's visiting her dad,' Jessica replied. 'She's going to stay with him until tomorrow night.' She took off her hat and shook her short blonde hair. 'Shall we get started on the project?'

Lauren nodded and they went to find Mel, who was in the tack room.

'We can do the project over there,' Mel said, pointing to a large wooden chest where the horses' brushes and clean saddlecloths were kept. It was covered in sheets of paper, horse books and felt-tip pens. 'I thought we could do some big posters.'

'That's a great idea,' Lauren agreed. 'You could do some cartoons on them.'

They settled down to work. Lauren and Jessica made a poster showing the different colours and breeds of horses, and Mel made another with funny cartoon drawings showing how *not* to look after a pony. In one cartoon there was a rider facing the wrong way; in another, someone was trying to groom a pony with a vacuum cleaner.

'These posters look really good,' Jessica said admiringly, after an hour.

Mel nodded. 'I'm still worried about doing our talk last, though. You know what the boys in the class are like when they get bored. They'll probably start acting really dumb.'

They exchanged worried looks.

'It'll be fine,' Lauren said, trying to be optimistic. 'The other groups might not have cartoons.'

Looking slightly reassured, Mel and Jessica went back to work on the posters.

Lauren felt nervous. She'd better be right!

★

At lunchtime, Lauren rode home. As she
took Twilight to his stable she heard
someone call her name. Her dad and
Max were waving to her from the new
skateboard area. It had been transformed.
Where once there had been just
concrete, there were now a low rail, a
small ramp, a steeper ramp and a couple
of milk crates arranged into a jump.

'What do you think, Lauren?' Mr
Foster called.

'It looks really good,' Lauren replied.

'We've just finished,' her dad said. 'Max
was about to try it out.'

'Watch me, Lauren! Watch!' Max
insisted.

Putting his helmet on, he set off

around the course. He was slightly
wobbly on his skateboard, but he
managed to get up both the ramps and
back down, only falling off once. He even
tried a jump where the board stayed as if
glued to his feet while he was in the air.

'That's an Ollie,' he called proudly. 'I'm

going to practise and practise until I'm as good as Steven and Leo. I want to learn how to do a kick flip next. That's when the board flips as you jump.' His eyes shone.

Lauren smiled. 'That's great, Max.'

She rode Twilight over to the fence and dismounted. 'I just don't get skateboarding at all,' she said quietly to him as she ran the stirrups up the leathers. 'I mean, so someone can jump and turn the board under their feet? What's the big deal?' She thought for a moment. 'I guess that's how some people must feel about riding horses,' she decided.

Untying Twilight, she turned him out. Then she began to rinse Twilight's feed buckets. It would be good to get them cleaned before she went inside.

'Come on, Max. Let's go get some lunch!' Mr Foster called.

Max and Mr Foster walked over to her.

'What did you think of my skating, Lauren?' Max asked eagerly.

'It looked great,' Lauren told him, emptying the water out of one of the buckets. It formed a muddy puddle on the ground.

Max stroked his skateboard lovingly, brushing away some tiny specks of dust. 'I can't wait to tell Steven and Leo about my new ramps!'

Just then there was a loud woof and Buddy came charging down the path.

'Mum must have let Buddy out,' Mr Foster said. 'Steady, boy!' he called to the excited dog.

But Buddy took no notice. He charged straight up to Max, his enormous paws splashing into the muddy puddle.

'Buddy! No!' Max gasped.

Lauren leapt back just in time. Water
went all over Max and his skateboard.

'Oh, Buddy!' Max yelled, looking at his
muddy skateboard. 'Look what you've
done!'

Five

Buddy sat down and thumped the tip of his tail uncertainly on the ground. 'I'm going to have to wash my skateboard now!' Max said crossly.

'It was an accident, Max,' said Mr Foster. 'Buddy didn't mean any harm. It's OK, Buddy.' Buddy jumped up and looked hopefully at Mr Foster. 'What is it, boy? You look like you want something.'

Buddy trotted forward and pushed his head against him.

'Max?' Mr Foster said suddenly. 'You have walked Buddy today, haven't you?'

'Um . . .' Max caught Lauren's eye. 'Well . . . not exactly,' he admitted. 'You see, I was busy and –'

'Max!' Mr Foster exclaimed. 'Poor Buddy. Go and take him for a walk right now.'

'But it's lunchtime!' Max protested.

'Well, you'll have to wait,' Mr Foster said firmly. 'Animals come first, and don't look at me like that,' he added as Max pulled a face. 'I'm very disappointed in you.'

'I'm sorry,' Max muttered. 'I suppose

I *should* have walked Buddy.'

Mr Foster nodded. 'Yes, you should.
You should take a leaf out of your sister's
book. She's always spending time with
Twilight, grooming him, feeding him,
noticing when there's something wrong.'
He smiled at her, but
Lauren felt a bit
awkward. Twilight was
easy to look after –
after all,

he could talk to her. And yes, she did spend a lot of time with him, but some of the time was when he was a unicorn. Her dad didn't know that!

'Go on, off you go,' Mr Foster said to Max. 'Lauren, are you coming in for lunch?'

Lauren hesitated. She felt sorry for Max. 'It's OK, Dad. I'll walk Buddy with Max.'

Max looked at her in surprise.

'OK,' Mr Foster shrugged. 'I'll see you both in the house when you get back.' He walked off.

'Dad's really annoying,' Max grumbled.

'He only told you off because he cares about Buddy,' she said as they set off down the path.

'Buddy's fine,' Max insisted.

'You *have* been neglecting him a bit,' Lauren ventured.

'I haven't!' Max said defensively. Buddy bounded over. 'See, he's happy.'

'Yes – now,' Lauren replied. 'But he looked really miserable this morning. You have to start paying him more attention, Max.'

'I do pay him attention!' Max protested. 'You're just fussing about nothing. Buddy's fine!'

'Yeah, right,' Lauren said. 'You forgot his supper yesterday, you didn't walk him today –'

'If you're going to nag me, I'll walk on my own,' Max said sulkily.

Lauren sighed. 'OK, let's not argue.'
Buddy trotted up to her and she stroked
his head. 'Come on, let's play hide and
seek with Buddy.'

Max nodded, cheering up. 'I'll hide
first.'

Hide and seek was one of Buddy's
favourite games. Max and Lauren took it
in turns to hide for Buddy to find them.

Then they had him jump over some low obstacles they made out of branches and fallen logs.

'This is fun!' Max exclaimed as he sprang over a small log with Buddy beside him.

'It is,' Lauren said, grinning.

After a while, they headed back to the farmhouse for lunch. Max was in a much better mood.

'Thanks for walking with me, Lauren,' he said. 'Sometimes it can be kind of lonely taking Buddy for walks.'

Lauren frowned. She hadn't thought about it before but it *must* be lonely for Max. She had Mel and Jessica to go riding with and even if they weren't there

Twilight could talk to her if she turned him into a unicorn. Max didn't have *anyone* to talk to when he was walking Buddy.

'It's a pity you haven't got any friends with dogs nearby,' she said. 'What about Steven and Leo? Do they like dogs?'

Max shrugged. 'I don't know. We only ever talk about skateboarding.' The farmhouse came into sight. 'Come on!' he exclaimed. 'I'll race you. I'm starving!'

For the rest of the afternoon, Lauren kept thinking about what Max had said. It was no wonder he was spending so much time with Steven and Leo; they were the only boys who lived within walking distance of the farm. Lauren hadn't thought about Max being lonely before and she wished there was a way to help him out.

'Can you think of anything we could do, Twilight?' she asked that evening when she turned him into a unicorn.

Twilight looked thoughtful. 'Maybe Max could come out on his bike with Buddy when we ride in the woods?'

Lauren considered it. 'Yes, and we could go out for picnics together. If I did more with Max, he might look after Buddy better.' She felt more cheerful. 'I'll ask him to come for a walk tomorrow.'

'That's a good idea.' Twilight nuzzled her. 'Come on, let's go flying now!'

CHAPTER

Six

The following morning, Lauren found Max in the kitchen with Buddy. 'Would you like to do something with Buddy and Twilight this morning?' she suggested. 'We could go into the woods. You could ride your bicycle and I could ride Twilight.'

'OK,' Max said eagerly.

'We can go after breakfast,' Lauren said,

putting a piece of bread in the toaster.

'I've had my breakfast,' Max said. Just then, the phone rang. Max picked it up. 'Granger's Farm,' he answered. A smile spread across his face. 'Hi, Steven. Yeah, I'd love to come over. You'll never guess what – Dad and I have built some ramps here!' There was a pause. 'OK. I'll go and ask my mum if I can come now.'

Max put the phone down. 'That was Steven,' he explained. 'He's invited me over so I won't be able to come to the woods with you.'

The kitchen door opened and Mrs Foster came in. 'Mum! Can I go to Steven and Leo's?' Max asked.

'Sure,' Mrs Foster said. 'But you have to

walk Buddy first.'

'Oh . . .' Max started to complain but he seemed to notice their mum's eyebrows raise. 'OK,' he sighed. 'I'll do it now.'

'Make sure it's a proper walk,' Mrs Foster added as he pulled on his trainers. 'Dad said you didn't walk him yesterday until lunchtime. That's not fair, Max. If you're going to have a dog you have to look after him properly. You know how strongly Dad and I feel about your pets being your responsibility.'

'I know,' Max shrugged. 'Come on, Buddy.'

He opened the door and Buddy bounded out.

'What are you going to do this morning, honey?' Mrs Foster asked Lauren as she put the kettle on.

'I think I'll call Mel and see if we can finish our project,' Lauren replied.

'Well, I'll be in my study if you need me,' Mrs Foster said. She made herself a cup of coffee and went back to work.

Lauren had only just finished her toast
when Max came back.

'Did you forget something?' she asked
in surprise.

'No, I've finished walking Buddy,' Max
replied.

'But that wasn't a long enough walk,'
Lauren said, looking at Buddy who was
standing hopefully by the door. 'You were
only out five minutes.'

'Yeah, but Steven said to come over
straight away,' Max said. 'I'll walk Buddy
again later. He'll be fine.' He grabbed his
skateboard. 'See you, Lauren!'

'Max!' Lauren started to protest, but the
door had already banged shut.

Buddy scratched at the door and

whined. Lauren walked over and stroked him. She could take him out for a walk herself but her mum or dad might see her, and then Max would get into trouble for not walking Buddy himself. And now she'd arranged to go to Mel's house to finish off their project. She couldn't leave Mel and Jessica to do it all on their own.

'I'll take you out at lunchtime if Max hasn't walked you properly,' she promised Buddy. She got out a dog chew from the cupboard. Buddy chewed it listlessly.

Lauren felt awful as she let herself out of the house. *Poor Buddy*, she thought as she hurried down the path to Twilight's field.

*

When Lauren got to Mel's house, the three girls decided to go for a ride in the woods before carrying on with their project.

'We could go to the creek and skim stones,' Mel suggested.

'Cool,' Jessica agreed.

Lauren nodded, but she couldn't get Buddy out of her thoughts. Was he still waiting by the door?

Mel and Jessica tacked up and they rode into the woods. After a while, Mel looked at Lauren. 'You're very quiet. Is everything OK?'

'I'm worried about Buddy,' Lauren admitted. 'Max isn't looking after him properly.' She told the others what was going on. 'If Mum and Dad find out he hasn't been walked today they'll be really mad, and Buddy's so unhappy.'

'Can't you say something to Max?' Jessica asked.

'I've tried, but he just says Buddy's happy and I'm worrying about nothing –'

She broke off with a gasp as something big, black and furry burst out of the

bushes beside them. The three ponies shied in alarm.

'Buddy!' Lauren exclaimed as the Bernese mountain dog skidded to a stop.

'Steady, Sandy!'

Hearing Jessica's alarmed cry, Lauren swung round. Sandy, who was young and easily startled, was racing backwards with her eyes rolling. Jessica had lost her stirrups.

'Hang on, Jess!' Mel cried out as Sandy half-reared up in fear. Jessica grabbed for a handful of mane, but she lost her grip and slipped off Sandy's back, landing on the ground with an uncomfortable thud.

'Whoa, Sandy!' Lauren cried as the palomino pony cantered towards her. She tried to grab Sandy's reins but her fingers closed around thin air.

In a thunder of hooves, Sandy galloped off down a side track into the trees.

'Sandy!' all three girls cried.

Mel looked round and, seeing Jessica still on the floor, leapt off Shadow. 'Jess? Are you OK?'

'I'm fine,' Jessica said, scrambling to her feet. 'But we've got to catch Sandy!'

Buddy trotted towards Shadow. Mel grabbed his collar.

'Twilight's the fastest. I'll go after Sandy!' Lauren said.

'OK,' Mel said.

Tears were streaking down Jessica's face. 'Please catch her, Lauren! *Please!*'

CHAPTER

Seven

Twilight needed no encouragement.
Plunging forward, he galloped in
the same direction as Sandy.

Lauren bent low over his neck, her heart
pounding. Where was Sandy? The pony
could go deeper and deeper into the woods
and get lost completely. Or maybe she'd
find her way on to a road. Or to the old
quarry with its steep dangerous sides . . .

'Oh, Twilight, we've got to catch her!'
Lauren gasped.

Twilight weaved in and out of the
trees. The forest grew thicker with every
stride. He started to slow down, every so
often jumping over a twisted tree root.
The trees were too close together for him
to gallop safely.

An image of Sandy lying injured filled
Lauren's mind. 'Twilight, please! Go as
fast as you can!' she begged.

To her surprise, Twilight stopped.
Lauren lurched forward on to his neck.
'What are you doing?' Twilight stamped
his front hoof and whinnied, and
suddenly Lauren knew what he was
trying to say. 'It'll be quicker if we fly?'

Twilight nodded.

Lauren glanced round. It was broad daylight and even though they were deep in the heart of the woods it would be really risky to turn Twilight into a unicorn now. Someone might see him. But they had to stop Sandy.

'OK,' she whispered. She quickly said the words of the Turning Spell.

In a second, Twilight was a unicorn.

'Sandy's gone this way,' he said. 'I can see her hoofprints and there are some cream-coloured hairs on that branch over there. She's heading towards the quarry but if I fly fast we might be able to cut her off!'

'Be as quick as you can,' Lauren
begged. 'Sandy could really hurt herself!'

Twilight plunged into the air and they
flew through the treetops, just skimming
the branches.

'There!' Lauren gasped, catching a
glimpse of gold through the trees. 'I think
I can see her!'

'I'll fly down,' Twilight said.

Lauren saw the deep jagged pit of the
quarry as they circled above it and then
Twilight swooped to the ground. As he
landed on a clear patch of rock, Lauren
heard the sound of Sandy's hooves.

'She's coming!'

Sandy burst out of the trees. Her eyes
were wide with fear. One of her stirrup

leathers had come off and her reins were trailing dangerously around her legs. She was heading straight for the edge of the quarry!

Twilight stepped on to the track and lifted his head. A ray of sunshine filtered through the leaves, lighting up his silver horn and making it sparkle.

With a snort, Sandy slowed down.

Twilight blew out softly and stepped towards her. Bending his head, he let his horn touch her neck. Lauren guessed that he was using his magic power to calm fear. As she watched, the terror gradually faded from Sandy's eyes. Her breathing slowed and she stopped trembling.

Slipping off Twilight's back, Lauren

walked up to the palomino pony. 'It's OK, girl,' she murmured, reaching out for the pony's reins.

Sandy whinnied. Twilight nickered back.

'What's she saying?' Lauren asked.

'She says she was really frightened by the dog jumping out,' Twilight

explained. 'She didn't realize it was
Buddy.'

'Oh, Sandy,' Lauren said, smoothing the
palomino's white forelock. 'You silly
thing. Come on, let's get you back to Mel
and Jessica.'

Twilight looked around. 'I guess you
should turn me back to a pony first,
Lauren. We're near the main track here
and someone might see me.'

Lauren said the words of the Undoing
Spell and remounted. Then, holding on
to Sandy's reins, she led her back through
the trees.

Mel and Jessica were waiting where Lauren
had left them. Jessica was crying. Mel had

one arm around her, with her other hand holding firmly on to Buddy's collar.

'Sandy!' Jessica cried when Lauren appeared with the ponies. She raced over. 'Is she OK?'

'Her reins are broken but she's fine,' Lauren replied, handing Sandy's reins to Jessica and dismounting.

Jessica flung her arms around her pony's neck and hugged her hard. 'Oh, Sandy, I was so worried.'

Sandy nuzzled her.

'She was just startled by Buddy,' Lauren explained. She caught herself quickly. 'I mean, I *think* that's why she galloped off.' She looked at Buddy. 'Buddy, what were you doing in the woods?'

Buddy panted, his tongue hanging out of his mouth. He looked like he was smiling, but Lauren saw him lick his lips and wag just the tip of his tail, two signs that he was feeling confused. 'Come on,' she sighed, stroking his ears. 'I'd better take you home.' She looked at Mel. 'I'll take Buddy back and then come over.'

'OK,' Mel agreed. 'We'll take Shadow and Sandy home.'

Lauren took Twilight's reins over his head and, holding on to Buddy's collar with one hand, she started to trudge home through the woods.

'I guess you were probably trying to find Max,' she said to the dog. 'Well, I hope I can get you back in the house without Mum or Dad seeing that you've been out on your own.'

But as she turned on to the track that led to Twilight's field, her heart sank. Her mum and dad were both near Twilight's stable, calling Buddy's name.

Pulling away from Lauren's hand, Buddy bounded down the track to meet them.

'Hey, where did you find Buddy?' Mr Foster asked in surprise.

'Er, he was in the woods,' Lauren replied. She decided not to mention the fact that Buddy had scared Sandy and made Jessica fall off.

'He escaped from the kitchen,' Mrs Foster said. 'I think he must have pressed

the handle down when he was pawing at the door. I saw him go past the study window, towards Twilight's stable. I called him but he didn't stop.' She shook her head. 'It's very strange. He never normally runs off. Max *did* walk him this morning, didn't he, Lauren?'

'Um . . .' Lauren really didn't want to

get Max into trouble. 'Yes. He . . . he *did* take him out.'

Mr Foster seemed to hear the hesitation in her voice. He looked at her shrewdly. 'For a proper walk?'

Lauren felt her cheeks go red. 'Not exactly.'

Mrs Foster looked angry. 'But I *told* Max he wasn't to go to Steven and Leo's until he'd walked Buddy.' She shook her head. 'I'm very cross with him. In fact, I'm going over there right now to bring him home.'

'Oh, Mum, please don't . . .' Lauren protested. She knew how embarrassed Max would be to have their mum turn up to drag him home.

'No, Lauren. Max has gone too far this

time. He's been neglecting Buddy ever since he started skateboarding.'

Lauren bit her lip as her mum and dad set off up the path.

'Oh, Twilight,' she whispered. 'Max is in real trouble now.'

Lauren waited with Twilight until she heard her mum's car coming back down the drive. Hurrying up the path, she saw Max getting out of the car. 'It's not fair,' he was shouting. 'Why did I have to come home?'

'You *know* why, Max,' Mrs Foster said, getting out too. 'I asked you to walk Buddy before you went to your friends and you didn't.'

'I did!'

'You didn't take him out for long enough. Lauren told us.'

Max glared at Lauren. 'Thanks, Lauren!'

'Don't take it out on your sister,' Mrs Foster scolded. 'You should have taken Buddy out for a proper walk. He escaped into the woods this morning. Anything could have happened.'

'But nothing did,' Max protested.

Lauren was very glad she hadn't mentioned Sandy's fall. Max and Buddy were in quite enough trouble already.

'That's not the point,' Mrs Foster said. 'Buddy's your responsibility, and if you can't look after him Dad and I are not going to let you keep him. We'll find him another home.'

'No!' Max gasped.

'Mum!' Lauren exclaimed.

'I mean it, Max,' Mrs Foster said firmly. 'I will *not* see an animal neglected.'

'But Buddy's not neglected.' Max

stamped his foot. 'You're not being fair!'

'Go to your bedroom please, Max.
We'll talk about this when you've calmed
down.'

Max ran into the house, slamming the
door behind him.

Lauren stared at her mum. 'Mum,
you wouldn't really give Buddy away,
would you?'

Mrs Foster ran a hand through her hair. 'I'm sorry, Lauren. I know you love Buddy. I do too. But I can't stand by and see Max make him unhappy.' She sighed. 'I just hope Max gets the message.'

Lauren looked up at her younger brother's bedroom window. *Oh, Max*, she thought. *Please start looking after Buddy properly. Please!*

CHAPTER

Eight

Lauren didn't sleep well that night.
She couldn't stop worrying about
Max. He had looked after Buddy for the
rest of the day, feeding him and brushing
him, but he had done it sulkily and
Lauren had noticed their mum frowning
as she watched him. *If only Buddy could
talk to him like Twilight can talk to me,*
Lauren thought as she turned over

restlessly in bed. *Then he'd be able to tell Max how he feels.*

The next day, Lauren found herself yawning as some of her classmates presented their projects. Even though she loved ponies, it was hard to pay attention when Jade's group began the second talk of the day on how to look after a pony.

'This is a dandy brush,' Jade said, pointing to a picture that was too small for the rest of the class to see. 'And this is a body brush.' She pointed to another picture. 'And this is a curry comb.'

'We've heard all this!' Adam Neil called out. 'David's group did horses this morning!'

'Tell us something different,' said

Adam's friend Simon. 'This is boring!'

'Settle down please, boys,' Mrs Bradshaw, their teacher said. 'Just listen.'

Mel shot Lauren a worried look. Lauren guessed what she was thinking. If people were bored now, how were they going to feel listening to a third presentation about horses? *We've got to make our talk more interesting*, she thought desperately. *But how?*

On the way home from school, Lauren, Max and Mrs Foster stopped at Mrs Fontana's shop so Mrs Foster could collect a book she had ordered.

The doorbell tinkled as they walked in and Walter, Mrs Fontana's terrier, trotted over to meet them.

'Hello,' Mrs Fontana said, appearing from the back of the old-fashioned shop. She was wearing a yellow shawl and her grey hair was held back in a bun. 'You must be here to pick up your book.'

'Yes, please,' Mrs Foster replied.

'Do you have any books on skateboarding, Mrs Fontana?' Max asked.

Mrs Fontana smiled. 'There's some in the children's section. Take a look if you want, Max.'

'Thanks,' Max said. He hurried to the back of the shop.

Mrs Fontana turned to Lauren. 'Lauren, would you mind giving me a hand in the storeroom? I put your mum's book on a high shelf, but my arthritis is playing up today and I would be very grateful if you would help me get it down.'

While her mum browsed, Lauren followed Mrs Fontana to the back of the shop and through a curtain of glass beads that glittered and sparkled. Lauren had never been in the storeroom before. The shelves that lined the narrow walls were packed with books, and there was a small desk in one corner.

'How's Twilight?' Mrs Fontana asked.

'Great,' Lauren replied. 'We discovered that he can untangle thorns with his magic.'

'Ah yes, that's the power he has to make order out of chaos,' Mrs Fontana nodded. 'Very useful.' She fetched a low stepladder. 'Your mother's book is on the second shelf. If you could just reach it down for me, that would be a great help.'

'Sure.' Lauren climbed up and took the book down.

Mrs Fontana smiled. 'Thank you, my dear.'

As she passed her the book, Lauren noticed how stiff Mrs Fontana's fingers were. 'Couldn't Twilight use his magic to cure your arthritis, Mrs Fontana?' she asked, thinking about how Twilight had once used his magic to heal cuts on her hands.

Mrs Fontana shook her head. 'My arthritis comes from old age. I'm afraid

even unicorn magic can't cure that.'

'Oh,' Lauren said.

Mrs Fontana's blue eyes studied Lauren. 'You look worried about something, my dear.'

'Two somethings actually,' Lauren admitted. 'A school project I'm doing, and Max.' She told Mrs Fontana everything that had been happening. 'It's awful,' she finished. 'Mum's serious about finding Buddy another home if Max doesn't start looking after him.' She looked hopefully at Mrs Fontana. 'There isn't anything Twilight and I can do, is there?'

'I'm afraid that this is one of those problems – just like my arthritis – that can't be solved by unicorn magic,' Mrs Fontana said. 'It sounds to me that Max has become so caught up in his new hobby that he's forgotten how much Buddy means to him and how much he means to Buddy. But neither you nor Twilight can make him realize that.'

Lauren sighed. 'The thing is, I *know* Max loves Buddy deep down. He just doesn't seem to understand what he's feeling.' She frowned. 'If only there was some way Buddy could speak to Max, like Twilight can talk to me.'

Mrs Fontana smiled. 'Oh, Lauren. All animals can talk. People just need to listen.'

'What do you mean?' Lauren asked.

Mrs Fontana's eyes crinkled up at the corners. 'You don't need me to explain. If you think about it, my dear, I'm sure you'll work it out on your own. And it might just help you with your problems too.'

Lauren didn't have time to ask Mrs

Fontana what she meant before they went back through the curtain into the shop.

Lauren's mum and Max were standing by the counter. 'We'd better get going,' said Mrs Foster.

Mrs Fontana rang up the purchase on the till. 'See you again soon,' she called as they left.

'Bye, Mrs Fontana,' Lauren replied. She was still thinking about what Mrs Fontana had said in the storeroom. *'All animals can talk. People just need to listen.' What did she mean? Animals couldn't talk. Well, apart from Twilight, and that was only because he was a unicorn.*

'I just don't get it,' she said as she groomed Twilight a little while later.

'Animals can't talk. What did Mrs
Fontana mean?'

Twilight stamped his hoof. Just then,
Lauren noticed a patch of mud on his
tummy just where his girth would go.
She started to brush at it quickly. Twilight
threw his head up and swished his tail.

'What's the matter?' Lauren asked. 'Was
I being too rough? Sorry.' She began to
brush more carefully, this time using
smooth gentle strokes.

Twilight relaxed and Lauren smiled.
Sometimes she didn't need him to be a
unicorn to understand what he was saying.

Her eyes widened.

'Of course! That's what Mrs Fontana
means!'

Twilight looked round at her.

'She *wasn't* saying that animals can speak to people like you talk to me when you're a unicorn. She meant that animals can communicate with people in other ways. Like when you put your ears back, I know that means you're unhappy, and

when you stamp your hoof, you're impatient.'

Twilight tossed his head.

A thought struck Lauren. 'And it's not just ponies, is it? Other animals can talk to people too. Maybe that's what Mrs Fontana meant about Max. If he can watch Buddy closely and understand what he's saying, he'll find it easier to look after him –' She broke off.

She'd just had the perfect idea for the school project!

CHAPTER

Nine

'What do you think?' Lauren asked, looking at Mel and Jessica a little while later. 'How about we do a project on how ponies talk to us?'

Mel and Jessica were staring at her as if they thought she'd gone crazy.

'But Lauren,' Jessica said, 'ponies don't talk.'

'They do!' Lauren insisted. 'Sure, they

don't open their mouths and speak
words, but they tell us what they're
thinking by the way they move their ears
and heads and tails. I think we should do
our project on how ponies –' she
searched for the right word – 'how they
communicate.'

Mel and Jessica still didn't look
convinced.

'Watch.' Lauren led Twilight over to
where Shadow was tied up. Shadow
pricked his ears and the two ponies
touched noses. 'They're saying hello.
Breathing out through their nostrils is
their way of greeting each other – or us.'
She walked up to Shadow and he
obligingly lifted his head and blew on to

her face. 'See, he's saying hello to me!'

'I guess so. I hadn't really thought about it as talking,' Mel said.

'I know, but that's what it is,' Lauren said. 'And I think the rest of our class would be really interested if we did our project on this.'

Jessica nodded. 'We could still use our posters and things, but if we did this as well it would be loads better than just doing another talk on how to look after a horse.'

'Yes,' Mel agreed. 'I know, how about we make a *video* of our ponies and show it to the class?'

'That's a great idea!' Lauren exclaimed. 'We could film the ponies doing different things and explain to the class what they're saying with their body language. We could even take some regular photos and get the class to guess what moods the ponies are in each picture.'

The three girls looked at each other excitedly.

'No one would be bored if we did that,' Mel said. 'I'll go and ask Mum if I can borrow our video camera.'

Luckily, Mrs Cassidy agreed and the three girls set about filming Shadow, Sandy and Twilight. Twilight was wonderful. He swished his tail when Lauren groomed his tummy, and put his ears forward and whickered when Lauren walked up to

him. He tossed his head when Lauren did
his girth up too tight, and stamped his
hoof when she rattled his feed bucket.

'It's like he understands what we want!'
Mel exclaimed.

Lauren hid a grin. There were some
definite advantages to Twilight being a
unicorn!

The girls worked until the sun was

setting and it was time for Lauren to ride home.

'I'll ask Mum to bring me back as soon as I've fed Twilight and turned him out in the field,' she promised.

'OK. We'll put Sandy and Shadow away and start looking at the video,' said Mel.

When Lauren reached Twilight's stable she saw Max practising on his skateboard. He was jumping in the air and trying to turn the board under his feet. Remembering that she'd been meaning to talk to him about Buddy, Lauren untacked Twilight and went to the gate. 'Max,' she called. 'Can I talk to you for a minute?'

'Not now,' Max replied. 'Steven and

Leo are coming over tomorrow and I
want to be able to do this kickflip
perfectly.' He turned his skateboard round
and tried again.

Lauren hesitated. *I'll talk to him later*,
she decided, and she went back to
Twilight.

But when Lauren finally got back from
Mel's house that night, it was eight thirty
and Max had already gone to bed.

I guess I'll just have to wait till the morning,
she decided. Kicking off her boots, she
headed upstairs to take a shower.

The next morning, Max was already up
and practising on his skateboard when

Lauren went outside to give Twilight his breakfast.

'Max!' Lauren called, waving to him. 'Come over here.'

'I can't,' Max replied. 'I'm practising.'

'I wanted to talk to you about Buddy,' Lauren said, going over to him. 'I don't think you understand what he's thinking a lot of the time, and that makes it hard for you to look after him.'

Max looked confused.

'Think about when he wags his tail,' Lauren persisted. 'Sometimes it means he's happy, but sometimes it means he's confused or worried. It depends *how* he wags his tail. There are other things as well, like how he pricks his ears and if he's panting or not. They're all ways he tries to talk to you.'

Max didn't look convinced. 'Yeah, right.' He got on his skateboard again.

'Max, this is important!' Lauren protested. 'I really can help you to understand Buddy better –'

'Some other time,' Max said, and he began to skate away from her.

Lauren watched him go, feeling frustrated, before heading back to the tack room. She needed to feed Twilight and get ready for school. Butterflies fluttered in her stomach at the thought of presenting their project that afternoon.

She mixed Twilight's feed and took it to the paddock. 'I hope the other kids like all the stuff we've done about horses,' she told him.

He lifted his head and snorted reassuringly. Bits of grain fell on to Lauren's jeans, but she didn't care. She knew he was just trying to tell her that everything would be fine. She hugged him.

'Thanks, Twilight,' she said, feeling better. 'I'll come and see you as soon as I get home to tell you all about it.'

She gave him a kiss, then climbed over the gate and hurried back to the house.

CHAPTER

Ten

Lauren, Jessica and Mel were the very last group to present their project. The previous talk had been on stick insects and even Mrs Bradshaw had looked as if she was having trouble staying awake.

'Well, it's time for the last presentation,' she announced, sounding relieved. 'Lauren, Mel, Jessica, would you come up please?'

'Not another talk on horses!' Adam complained.

'Oh no,' Simon groaned.

'Well, it's not just a talk about how to look after a horse,' said Lauren as she walked up to the front with Mel and Jessica following. 'It's about how horses communicate.'

'Yes,' Jessica backed her up. 'And how people can tell what horses are thinking.'

The class looked more interested.

'OK,' Mrs Bradshaw said. 'Now, you told me you'd like to use the video recorder. It's all set up, so when you're ready, you can start.'

'Cool! We get to watch TV,' Adam said, looking more cheerful.

Lauren exchanged looks with Mel and Jessica. They had agreed that she would start. Taking a deep breath, she smiled at the class. 'Our project is called "Animals can talk, if only people listen". We're going to show you how ponies communicate and how easy it is to understand what they're trying to say.' She glanced at Mel. 'Mel, can you start the video please?'

To Lauren, Jessica and Mel's relief, their talk was a great success. The whole class listened while they showed them the video and talked about what the ponies were doing. Then Jessica gave out the photos they'd printed and they split the

class into groups to guess the ponies'
moods.

There was a picture of Twilight with
his ears back, one of Sandy pawing the
ground, one of Shadow with his ears
pricked in excitement and a picture of
Twilight nuzzling Lauren affectionately.

Even Adam and Simon joined in and
called out suggestions. Mel finished by

holding up her posters. Everyone loved Mel's cartoons and Mrs Bradshaw said she would stick them up on the classroom wall.

'That was a fascinating project!' she said when the girls had finished. 'You should be very proud of yourselves – and your ponies. They posed beautifully for the photos and it was clear exactly what they were saying.'

'It was cool!' Adam called out.

Someone started to clap and the whole class joined in. Lauren, Mel and Jessica blushed and exchanged pleased smiles.

Just then the bell rang. With the sound of the applause still ringing in their ears, the three girls headed for the cloakroom.

'I can't believe it went so well!' Mel exclaimed.

'You were great, Lauren,' Jessica said. 'You explained everything perfectly.'

Lauren grinned. She felt proud but also very relieved. It was over and it had been a success. She couldn't wait to get home and tell Twilight all about it!

When she went into the schoolyard she was surprised to see Steven and Leo standing with Max; then she remembered that they were coming home with him to play.

All the way back to the farm, the boys talked about skateboarding.

As soon as Mrs Foster pulled up

outside the farmhouse, Max jumped out
of the car. 'The ramps are this way!'

'Max!' Mrs Foster said. 'Maybe Steven
and Leo want to get a drink first.'

'We're fine, thanks,' Steven said politely.
'Aren't we, Leo?'

Leo nodded. 'We'd really love to see the
skateboard stuff, Mrs Foster.'

'OK,' Mrs Foster said, smiling. 'Off
you go!'

The boys grabbed their skateboards and helmets and hurried off. Mrs Foster turned to Lauren. 'Steven and Leo are nice, aren't they?'

Lauren nodded. 'Yeah, though a bit skateboard mad. I thought Max was bad enough!'

Mrs Foster headed for the house. 'Are you coming in?'

'I'll just go see Twilight first,' Lauren replied. She ran down the track towards Twilight's paddock. He was waiting at the gate.

'Hi, boy,' Lauren said, patting him. 'The project was great! Everyone loved the video.'

On the other side of the field, the boys

were already on their skateboards. 'Watch this!' Max called. He jumped in the air and flipped his board.

'Way to go!' Steven said.

Max looked very proud. 'I can do a kick flip after coming down a ramp, too.'

'Are you sure, Max?' Leo said. 'That's really difficult.'

'Yeah,' Steven said doubtfully. 'You haven't been skating that long.'

'Watch!' Max insisted. He skated up to the highest ramp.

Just then, there was the sound of thundering paws. Lauren turned to see Buddy charging down the path from the house. He galloped straight towards Max just as he started coming down the ramp, his face frowning in concentration.

Max looked up in alarm as Buddy woofed, and his skateboard wobbled. Max's arms flailed wildly, but it was too late and the skateboard flipped over.

'Oh no!' Lauren gasped as Max crashed to the ground. She ran to the fence. 'Are you OK, Max?'

Buddy jumped on top of Max, his tail wagging like mad.

'I'm fine. Get off, Buddy!' Max shouted. 'You stupid dumb dog!' He clambered to his feet. His cheeks were bright red with embarrassment.

'Are you sure you're all right?' Steven said hurrying over to him. 'That was a bad fall.'

'It was a really difficult move to try,' Leo agreed. 'Especially since you haven't been skateboarding that long.'

Lauren saw tears of humiliation in her brother's eyes. 'I'd have been fine if it hadn't been for Buddy. I only fell off because of him.' He turned on Buddy. 'I hate you! You always wreck everything. Well, I hope Mum and Dad do give you away after all!'

With that he turned and ran into the house.

There was an awkward silence. Buddy sat down and whined.

'Oh, Buddy,' Lauren said, climbing the fence. Buddy came trotting over to her and thrust his nose into her hand.

Steven looked at his younger brother. 'You shouldn't have said that, Leo. You made it sound like Max was just a little kid. He might have managed the jump if he hadn't been distracted by the dog.'

Leo looked awkward. 'I just meant it was a difficult jump for a beginner.' He looked at Lauren. 'I didn't mean to upset Max.'

Lauren sighed. 'Don't worry. I think he was just embarrassed about falling off.'

Steven walked over to her. 'Is this your dog?'

'No, he's Max's,' Lauren replied. 'Hasn't Max ever told you about him?'

'No,' Steven replied. 'But then we always just talk about skateboarding. He stroked Buddy's head. 'Hi there, fella.'

Buddy's tail thumped on the ground.

Leo started petting him too. Buddy
jumped up and pushed against Leo's legs,
almost knocking him over. Leo laughed.

'What should we do about Max?'
Steven said.

'I don't think there's anything you *can*
do,' Lauren said. 'It's best to give him a
chance to calm down. I'll go see him in a
minute.'

'I guess we should go home then,'
Steven said to Leo. 'It doesn't seem right
to practise on Max's ramps without him.'

'Will your mum or dad be home?'
Lauren asked.

'Mum will,' Steven replied. 'Tell Max to

come and find us if he wants. He can
bring his skateboard over.'

The two boys gave Buddy one last pat
and set off. Buddy made as if to follow
them but Lauren grabbed his collar. 'No,
you don't, Buddy.'

Buddy whimpered and tried to pull
after the boys.

Lauren sighed. She knew she should go
see how Max was. She walked up to the
house with Buddy. When she got to the
back door she stopped. 'Maybe you
should wait here, Buddy. I'm not sure
Max will want to see you at the
moment.' She could still hear Max's
words ringing in her ears. *I hate you! I
hope Mum and Dad do give you away.* She
was sure Max had only said those
things because he'd been feeling
humiliated. But what sort of mood
would he be in now?

As she reached the top of the stairs she
heard the sound of Max crying.

'Max?' Lauren said, pushing his
bedroom door open. 'Max? Are you OK?'

Her brother was lying on his bed. 'Go
away!'

'Max, don't cry. There's nothing to be
upset about.'

'Yes there is. Steven and Leo just think
I'm a dorky little kid.'

'No they don't,' Lauren protested,
going and sitting on his bed.

'They do. I fell off my skateboard.'

'So? I'm sure everyone falls off,' Lauren
told him. 'It's like horse riding. The
important thing is that you get back up
and try again.'

'I guess,' Max muttered. He sniffed. 'I
just wish Leo and Steven hadn't been
there. I feel so stupid.'

'Don't worry,' Lauren said. 'Leo and

Steven won't care about you falling off.
They're your friends. It's like Jessica and
Mel. They don't laugh at me if I make
mistakes on Twilight. They make me feel
better.'

There was a silence as Max thought
about what she'd said. 'Really?'

'Really,' Lauren told him.

The tears started to dry on Max's face. 'Where are Leo and Steven now?'

'They went home. I think they felt a bit awkward,' Lauren replied. 'But they told me to tell you to go round and see them. They said to bring your skateboard.'

'So they *do* still want to be friends with me?' Max asked.

Lauren nodded.

Max looked relieved. 'I'll go over right now,' he said, getting up and heading for the door.

'Max,' Lauren said. He stopped and looked at her. 'You weren't very nice to Buddy just now,' she told him. 'He didn't mean any harm. He was just excited to see you. If you'd gone to see him when you got home, he wouldn't have come racing out like that.'

Max hesitated. 'I guess.' He looked rather shamefaced. 'I didn't really mean those things I said, you know.'

'I know, but it upset Buddy,' Lauren told him. 'He couldn't understand why you were shouting at him just for saying hello.'

Max bit his lip. 'All right. I'll tell him everything's OK. Where is he?'

'Outside,' Lauren replied.

They went down to the kitchen.

'Buddy! Here, boy!' Max called, opening the door.

But Buddy didn't appear.

'Buddy! Where are you?' Max called again.

Lauren fetched Buddy's tin bowl and banged it. It was a sound that usually made Buddy come running. But not this time.

'Where is he?' Max frowned.

'I don't know,' said Lauren, starting to feel worried. 'I left him here.'

'It's not like Buddy to wander off,' Max said. 'Maybe it's because I shouted at him.' His eyes widened and his face went pale. 'Oh, Lauren!' he exclaimed. 'Do you think he's run away?'

CHAPTER
Eleven

Lauren stared at her brother. 'Run away?'

'I said I hated him!' Max burst out. 'I said I didn't want him any more. He might have thought I meant it!' He ran outside. 'Buddy!' he called. 'Come back. I didn't mean any of those things!'

But still no Buddy.

Tears started to well in Max's eyes. 'Buddy! *Buddy!*'

Lauren felt her heart beat faster. 'We'd better tell Mum,' she said. 'Come on!'

Mrs Foster was very concerned to hear that Buddy had disappeared. 'He didn't even come back when you banged his food bowl?' she asked Lauren.

Lauren shook her head.

'I said I hated him, Mum. He's run away and it's all my fault!' Max said, tears running down his face.

'Calm down, Max,' Mrs Foster said. 'Buddy wouldn't run away just because of something you said.'

'I bet he would!' Max said, his words

coming out in a sob. 'He thinks I don't want him, but I do!'

'Do you want me to go and look in the woods with Twilight?' Lauren offered.

'Thanks, honey,' Mrs Foster said. 'I'll tell your dad and we'll search here on the farm.'

Lauren gave Max a quick hug. 'We'll find Buddy. Don't worry!'

She raced down the path. If she could just get Twilight into the woods and turn him into a unicorn, she could use his magic to find out where Buddy was. When Twilight touched his horn to rose quartz he could see anyone he wanted, *and* see where they were.

Twilight whinnied when he saw her.

'Buddy's disappeared,' Lauren told him. 'You didn't see him go, did you?'

Twilight shook his head.

'We've got to find him,' Lauren said. 'Let's go to the clearing in the woods so you can use your magic to look for him!'

She put Twilight's bridle on but didn't bother with his saddle. 'Come on!' she said, leading him out of the field and swinging herself on to his back.

As Twilight cantered into the woods, Lauren clung to his mane. Riding him bareback was much easier when he was in his magical shape and he had unicorn magic to keep her on!

Twilight leapt over a tree root in the path.

'Steady, boy!' Lauren gasped.

Just then, she heard the faint sound of barking. 'That sounds like Buddy!' she exclaimed.

She looked and looked, but the trees were so thick she couldn't see anything. She hesitated. Should they follow the noise or keep going to the clearing?

Woof! Woof! The bark was faint but it *definitely* sounded like Buddy. Twilight pulled towards the trees.

Lauren made up her mind. 'OK, Twilight. If you think it's Buddy, let's go that way.'

Twilight started to weave in and out of the trees as the path faded away. Ducking under branches, Lauren felt her heart pounding. Where was Buddy?

She remembered how he'd spooked Sandy and made her run off. What if he caused another accident? What if he was in an accident himself? An icy shiver ran down her spine.

The woofing was coming from the

edge of the woods where there were houses – and a road.

'Hurry, Twilight!' Lauren urged, feeling sick with worry.

Suddenly Twilight stopped. There was a low fence ahead marking out the boundary between the woods and the gardens behind the houses. But a deep thicket of blackberry bushes blocked the way to the fence.

'Oh no!' Lauren exclaimed in dismay.

She heard another bark. It seemed to come from just the other side of the fence. *Oh Buddy*, Lauren thought desperately. *Please don't be in trouble!*

'We'll have to go back,' she told Twilight. 'We can't get through this

way.' But to her
surprise Twilight
didn't move when
she pulled his
mane. 'Twilight!' she
exclaimed.

Twilight tossed up
his head and
stamped his hoof.

Lauren frowned. She
had a feeling he was trying to tell her
something. But what?

Twilight pushed at the bushes with his
nose.

In a flash, Lauren realized what he'd
been trying to say. *His magic powers!* He
could try to use them to untangle the

blackberry branches! 'You want me to turn you into a unicorn?'

Twilight nodded.

Lauren looked around. She was desperate to get to Buddy but it was very risky to turn Twilight into a unicorn in broad daylight. Still, the trees were really thick between her and the houses. She decided to take the risk.

Scrambling off Twilight's back, she said the magic words.

In a flash, Twilight turned into a unicorn. 'I can use my magic to try and clear a path by untangling the brambles,' he explained.

'Do you think it will work?' Lauren asked. These bushes were much thicker

than the place where the squirrel had
been trapped.

Twilight looked determined, and his
horn glowed even brighter. 'I'll try!'

He lowered his horn to the branches
and, sure enough, the briars started to
unravel! Twilight took a step forward,
touching his horn to the next tangle of
branches. Little by little, a narrow
pathway appeared.

'You're doing it, Twilight!' Lauren cried
in delight.

As the last brambles unwound
themselves, Lauren's impatience got the
better of her and she forced her way
through. Ignoring the scratches on her
arms, she ran to the fence and peered over.

'Twilight! It *is* Buddy!'

The fence bordered a long garden with a large house at the far end. Near the house was a hard tennis court with various pieces of skateboarding equipment on it – a ramp, a quarter pipe and several jumps. Two boys were rolling around on skateboards and, playing with them and woofing excitedly, was Buddy!

Lauren felt a wave of relief rush through her. Buddy was safe. He wasn't on the road and he wasn't in trouble.

'It's Leo and Steven,' Twilight said, joining Lauren at the fence. 'This must be their house.'

'I wonder what Buddy's doing here?' Lauren said.

'Maybe he got bored waiting outside your house and decided to follow Leo and Steven home?' Twilight suggested.

Lauren nodded. She felt trembly with relief. 'I'm so glad he's not in trouble. Should we go into the garden and get him? The fence is only low. You could easily jump it.'

'OK,' Twilight agreed. 'But you'd better change me back first.'

Lauren grinned. 'Yes. I think I'd better.' Steven and Leo seemed to like dogs but she had a feeling they'd be a bit surprised to see a real live unicorn in their garden!

She said the Undoing Spell and cantered Twilight up to the fence. He leapt over it easily.

The boys looked round. Seeing
Lauren and Twilight, Buddy barked
joyfully and ran over. 'Oh, Buddy,'
Lauren said, getting off Twilight and
hugging him. 'We've been so worried
about you!'

'How did you get here?' Steven asked
in surprise.

'I jumped over the fence,' Lauren said.

'I was looking for Buddy in the woods and I heard him barking.'

'But what about the blackberry bushes?' Steven asked. 'They're really thick on the other side of the fence.'

'Oh, I found a way through,' Lauren said quickly. 'How long has Buddy been here?'

'He arrived about ten minutes ago,' said Leo. 'He came trotting into the garden as if he wanted to come and play with us.'

'Max will be so pleased to know he's safe,' Lauren said. 'I should go and tell him Buddy's here.'

'Or I could ring Max and let him know right away,' Steven suggested.

'Yes please!' Lauren replied.

Steven set off towards the house. Leo stroked Twilight. 'He's lovely.'

'Thanks,' Lauren smiled. 'Do you like animals?'

'I love them,' Leo said. 'Steven does too. We used to have a dog, a golden retriever called Jake, but he died last year. It's been really weird without him.' He brightened

up slightly. 'But Mum and Dad say we can get another dog now we've moved to the country. Maybe it could be friends with Buddy.'

'Yeah!' Lauren exclaimed. 'That would be great!'

Buddy wagged his tail and woofed.

★

Five minutes later, there was the sound of a car on the drive and Max came tearing into the garden. 'Buddy!'

Buddy charged over to him. He stopped too late and almost sent Max flying, but Max didn't care. He flung his arms around the dog. 'Buddy, I'm so glad you're all right. I promise I'll never be mean to you again.'

Buddy licked his face. 'Yuk!' Max exclaimed, but then he laughed and hugged him even harder.

Mrs Foster came round the corner. 'Hello, Steven. Hello, Leo. I'm very glad you found Buddy.'

'Well, actually he found us,' Steven said.

'Whichever way round it was, I'm just glad he's safe,' Mrs Foster replied. She looked at Lauren. 'You did well to track him down.'

Lauren smiled. 'Twilight helped.'

Twilight snorted proudly.

'You know, sometimes I'm sure Twilight can understand every word you say,' Mrs Foster commented.

Lauren stroked Twilight to hide her grin.

'Come on, Max. Shall we take Buddy home?' said Mrs Foster.

Lauren saw Leo's and Steven's faces fall. 'Couldn't Max and Buddy stay here for a while?' she said.

'Yes please!' Steven exclaimed.

'But I haven't got my skateboard,' Max said.

'That's fine. We can play with Buddy instead,' said Steven.

Buddy woofed.

'We love dogs!' Steven told Max. 'We're going to get a puppy soon.'

'We'll be able to take our new dog and Buddy for walks together,' Leo added.

Max looked delighted. 'Cool!'

'Come on,' urged Steven. 'I bet Buddy will love running up and down the ramps and doing the jumps.'

'I'll come back in an hour,' Mrs Foster told Max.

'OK. See you later, Mum!' Max called, and he ran off after Leo and Steven with

Buddy bounding around them.

'See you at home, Lauren,' said Mrs Foster.

Lauren nodded and got back on Twilight. The boys were charging about the skateboard course with Buddy beside them. Lauren watched for a moment.

'I'm glad it's all worked out OK,' she murmured to Twilight.

He whickered in agreement.

'Come on,' she said softly. 'Let's go home.'

As they started up the garden, Max ran over. 'Lauren? Thanks for finding Buddy. I'm never going to be mean to him ever again.'

'Good,' Lauren smiled.

Max hesitated. 'And . . . um . . . you know what you were saying this morning, about how I can learn to tell what Buddy's thinking, by looking at his tail and ears? Well, will you help me learn that stuff?' He looked hopefully at Lauren. 'I'd really like to know what Buddy's saying.'

'Of course I'll help you,' Lauren told him.

'Thanks. I want to make him happy,' Max vowed. 'When I thought he'd run away, it was awful.'

Lauren glanced across to where Buddy was playing with Leo and Steven. 'He sure looks happy now.'

Max grinned. 'He does, doesn't he? I'll

see you later, Lauren!' And with that, he
ran back to join the others.

Lauren rode Twilight towards the fence.
He cleared it easily again.

As the trees closed around them,
Lauren slipped off his back and said the
Turning Spell. With a purple flash,
Twilight turned into a unicorn.

'We did it,' he said in delight. 'We found Buddy!'

'Yes, and it looks like Max isn't going to find it so lonely looking after him from now on.' Lauren leaned her head against Twilight's neck and breathed in his warm sweet smell. 'Thanks for helping, Twilight.'

'That's OK.' Twilight nuzzled her.

'I love you, Twilight,' Lauren whispered, hugging him hard.

They stood there for a moment, and then Lauren said the Undoing Spell. Twilight turned back into a pony and, climbing on to his back, Lauren rode him through the trees.

As the dusk gathered around them and

Twilight's hooves thudded on the forest floor, Lauren felt as if they were lost in their own private little world. She looked at Twilight's pricked ears. She knew she'd love him even if he couldn't talk, even if he was just a regular pony.

All ponies are special, she thought to herself. *And they can all talk to us if we just listen.*

She stroked Twilight's neck and smiled. All ponies *were* special, but unicorns were very special indeed.

My Secret Unicorn

Snowy Dreams

Twilight's magic was fading! Lauren
couldn't believe it. No more magic. No
more flying. And maybe soon, no more
talking to her best friend.

But the worst thing of all was how
unhappy this was making Twilight. Did he
really think she wouldn't love him
any more, just because he wasn't a
unicorn?

To Jessica Duxbury,
a very special friend

Prologue

In a distant land, three Unicorn Elders stood beside a stone table. Their silvery manes swept to the floor and their snow-white coats gleamed in the moonlight. One had a golden horn, one had a silver and the third had a bronze.

'It is time for us to find out,' the silver-horned unicorn said softly.

The other two unicorns nodded their noble heads.

The first unicorn touched the table top with her silver horn. Purple smoke began to drift across the surface and the stone shone like a mirror. An image appeared. It showed a small grey pony grazing in a field near a farmhouse at night-time. Behind the farm, almost hidden in shadow, rose the Blue Ridge Mountains of Virginia.

'It's Twilight,' the bronze-horned unicorn said slowly.

The three unicorns exchanged looks.

'I am surprised,' remarked the unicorn with the golden horn. 'Twilight is very young.' His voice sounded troubled.

The bronze-horned unicorn nodded.

'He is, and he has not been with his unicorn friend for long. But they have done many good things together – more than some unicorns and their friends do in many years.'

'That is true.' The unicorn with the golden horn looked at the others. 'I wonder how Twilight will take the news.'

'It is never easy,' the silver-horned unicorn said quietly. Her dark eyes, shimmering like deep pools, watched Twilight for a moment. 'I will go and tell him.'

'When will you go, Sidra?' the other unicorns asked.

Sidra lifted her head, her horn glittering in the starlight. 'Tonight.'

CHAPTER

One

Beep-beep-beep! Lauren Foster rubbed her eyes. Her alarm clock went off again. *Beep-beep-beep!* Fumbling at the side of her bed, she pressed the off-switch on the clock then sank back against her pillows. *What day is it?* she wondered sleepily.

Saturday! And not just any old Saturday but the first day of the Christmas

holidays! Lauren suddenly felt wide
awake. She didn't have to go to school for
over two whole weeks and she could
spend every day with Twilight!

Jumping out of bed, she padded over to
the window. Pulling the curtains open,
she saw Twilight standing by his paddock
gate and she smiled. The day she had got
Twilight had been the best day of her
life. *Well, almost*, she thought,
remembering the time a few weeks after
that when she had found out that
Twilight wasn't just an ordinary pony –
he was a secret unicorn! Now, when
Lauren's parents and little brother, Max,
were sleeping, she turned Twilight into
his magical unicorn shape so that they

could go flying and do good deeds using
his magical powers. Lauren knew she was
really lucky to have a pony, and she was
even luckier to have a unicorn as well!

Twilight began to walk along by the
fence. Reaching the end of the field, he
turned and paced back again. Lauren

frowned. It wasn't like Twilight to be so restless. He usually waited patiently by the gate. *He must be hungry*, she decided.

Turning from the window, she pulled on her jeans and warm sweatshirt. As she got dressed, she planned the morning in her head. She'd feed Twilight his breakfast and then groom him. At nine thirty, Mel and Jessica, her two best friends, were coming over on their ponies to go for a ride in the woods. The weekend before, the three of them had discovered a large clearing in the trees with banks and steep slopes. They'd had great fun riding there and had decided to go back again.

Today's going to be brilliant! Lauren thought. Tying her long fair hair back in a ponytail, she hurried downstairs.

The rest of the house was quiet. Her dad's boots weren't on the porch so Lauren guessed he was out working on the family's farm. Buddy, Max's young Bernese mountain dog, jumped up when he saw her. She stopped to scratch his ears. 'Max will be up soon,' she told him.

Buddy wagged his tail and licked her hand. Grabbing an apple from the bowl, Lauren ran out of the house and down the frosty path to Twilight's field.

'Twilight!' she called.

Twilight stopped walking and looked round.

'Hi, boy!'

Whinnying, Twilight trotted to the

gate. When he reached it, he pushed his head against her, almost knocking her over.

'Steady!' Lauren laughed. 'Yes, the apple's for you. Here you go.'

But to her surprise, Twilight ignored the apple. Instead, he whickered and touched her hair and then her face with his muzzle.

'Are you OK?' Lauren asked.

Twilight stood still.

'Twilight?' Lauren said, feeling alarmed. 'Is something the matter?'

To her relief, Twilight shook his head.

He could understand Lauren when he was a pony and talk back to her in his own way, but now Lauren wished he could speak to her properly, with words, like he did when he was a unicorn. She wanted to find out why he seemed so uneasy. 'Are you feeling upset because I didn't come to see you last night?' she guessed. 'I'm sorry, but Mum and Dad had friends over for supper and I fell asleep before they went to bed. We can go flying tonight, I promise.'

But her words didn't seem to make Twilight any happier. He nudged her with his muzzle again. Lauren frowned. He was OK, wasn't he?

Of course he is, she thought. She'd asked him if there was anything wrong and he'd said no. Pushing her concerns away, she stroked his tangled mane. Time to get a

move on. He needed a good groom
before Jessica and Mel arrived!

By half past nine, Twilight's grey coat was
spotless, his long tail and mane were
brushed out and his hooves were shining
with hoof oil. But he still seemed restless,
and Lauren couldn't shake off the feeling

that there was something bothering him.

She had just finished tacking him up
when Mel and Jessica rode down the
path on Shadow and Sandy.

Lauren waved. 'Hi!'

'Twilight looks clean,' Jessica
commented.

'Pity about you, Lauren!' Mel grinned.

Lauren looked down at her clothes,
which were very dusty after brushing
Twilight, and grinned back. 'Never mind.
Twilight's the one that matters!'

The three ponies touched noses to say
hello. They were almost as good friends as
Mel, Jessica and Lauren were. Lauren
took hold of the reins and swung herself
into the saddle. 'Let's go!'

They rode down the path into the woods. It was a bright cold morning and the winter sun shone through the treetops, melting the frost on the ground. As soon as the track widened out, the ponies began to pull at their bits.

'I think Sandy wants to canter,' Jessica said, patting the young palomino pony's neck.

'What are we waiting for?' Mel shortened her reins as Shadow tossed his grey head. 'Come on!'

Eventually they reached the clearing. It was a hilly area with lots of bushes and twisty paths leading up and down banks and steep slopes. At first, Lauren, Mel and

Jessica rode cautiously but they soon
grew in confidence and began to try the
banks at a trot and a canter.

'What about that hill?' Mel suggested,
pointing to a high bank that none of
them had ridden down yet.

'No way,' Jessica said. 'It's much too
steep.'

Lauren was standing a little way off
with Twilight. 'What do you think,
Twilight?' Twilight was startled when he
heard his name and Lauren had the
feeling she'd interrupted his thoughts.
'Should we go down it?'

Twilight shook his head. 'We're not
going to do it either,' Lauren called to the
others.

'I've got an idea!' Mel said. 'Let's set a course over the rest of the clearing and then we can time ourselves and see who's the fastest.'

It was great fun but Twilight didn't seem to be as lively as usual. He stumbled several times and once or twice Lauren had to press him on, when normally she had to try and slow him down.

'Are you sure you're all right, Twilight?' she whispered, reining him in.

Twilight nodded but Lauren wasn't convinced. *I'll ask him what's wrong when I turn him into a unicorn tonight*, she decided. *We'll be able to talk properly then.*

CHAPTER

Two

As soon as her parents went to bed that evening, Lauren slipped out of the house. The night air was freezing on her skin and the farm was quiet. Excitement surged through her as she ran down the dark path. Soon she and Twilight would be flying. She could almost feel the wind whipping through her hair, feel the warmth of Twilight's

smooth back. What would they do
tonight? Maybe they'd go to the woods
and see what animals were around, or
maybe jump over the treetops . . .

If Twilight's feeling OK, she reminded
herself, thinking how oddly he'd been
behaving that day.

'Twilight!' she called softly.

He whinnied.

Lauren reached the gate and quickly
spoke the words of the Turning Spell.

'Twilight Star, Twilight Star,
Twinkling high above so far.
Shining light, shining bright,
Will you grant my wish tonight?
Let my little horse forlorn
Be at last a unicorn!'

There was a flash of purple light and
Twilight was transformed from a pony
into a unicorn. His grey coat gleamed
snow-white, his mane and tail hung in
silky strands and in the centre of his

forehead was a sparkling silver horn.

He stepped forward. 'Hello, Lauren.'

His mouth didn't move but Lauren could hear his voice clearly in her head so long as she was touching him or holding a hair from his mane. Nowadays, she made sure that she had one of his hairs with her at all times in case she needed to turn him into a unicorn and speak to him. 'Are you all right?' she asked, stroking his forelock.

'I'm fine,' Twilight said, but he let out a long sigh.

Lauren wondered why he seemed so down. *Maybe if we go flying it will cheer him up.* 'Do you want to go flying?' she suggested.

Twilight shook his head. 'No. I don't feel like it.'

Lauren was astonished. 'Why not?' The only time she'd ever known Twilight turn down the chance to go flying had been when he had been ill.

'I feel really tired after all the cantering and jumping today,' Twilight replied.

'OK,' Lauren said slowly. 'I suppose we can always go tomorrow instead.' She put her arms round his neck, feeling confused. It was not like Twilight to refuse a chance to go flying.

Another long sad sigh trembled through him.

'Twilight, what is it?' Lauren said, stepping back and looking at him.

'Something's wrong, I know it is. Are you
ill? Maybe I should get the vet?'

'No,' Twilight said. 'I don't feel ill. I'm . . .
tired.' He saw her concerned expression.
'I really don't feel ill. I'd tell you if I did, I
promise. I think I just need to rest. Will
you turn me back into a pony, please?'

Lauren stroked him worriedly. Twilight
wasn't behaving like himself at all. But what
could she do? 'OK,' she said and, giving
him a kiss, she said the Undoing Spell.

'Good night,' she murmured as the
purple flash faded and Twilight looked
like an ordinary pony once again.

Twilight whickered softly and Lauren
headed back towards the house, hoping
he'd feel better in the morning.

✶

Lauren got up early the next day to
check on Twilight. To her relief he
whinnied cheerfully when he saw her.

'Are you feeling better?' she asked.

Twilight nodded.

He definitely seemed livelier. He was
holding his head high and his eyes had
lost their worried look. Lauren felt

relieved. Perhaps he *had* just been tired the night before.

'We can go out for a ride later,' she told him.

After they had both had breakfast and Lauren had groomed Twilight, she tacked him up and rode into the woods. She decided to ride to the clearing with the banks and hills again. It was different riding there on her own, instead of with Mel and Jessica, but Lauren didn't mind. It was another crisp cold morning and it was great to be with Twilight, trotting along the frosty tracks. Everything was quiet, still and peaceful.

When they reached the clearing, Lauren saw that there were two other

riders already there. The girls looked a
few years older than her – maybe twelve
or thirteen. They were cantering down
the banks on their ponies, shouting to
each other. Lauren halted, not sure if she
should join in.

'Perhaps we should go back,' she
murmured to Twilight. But then one of
the girls' horses – a pretty bay Arab with
four white socks – noticed them. She
lifted her head and whinnied. Both girls
looked round.

'Hi there!' called the girl on the bay
mare. She had blonde hair tied in a short
stubby ponytail under her riding hat.

'Hi,' Lauren said shyly.

'Were you coming to ride here?' the

girl asked, riding over.

Lauren nodded. 'But it doesn't matter. I can come back another day.'

'No, it's OK,' the girl said. 'We don't mind. There's room for all of us. My name's Jo-Ann, by the way. And this is my pony, Beauty.'

Lauren looked at the pretty bay mare with her dished face and large dark eyes. 'She is beautiful.'

'Thanks,' Jo-Ann smiled. 'So, what's
your name?'

'Lauren. And this is Twilight.'

The other girl came over. 'I'm Grace,'
she said. 'And this is Windfall,' she added,
patting the neck of her chestnut pony.

'Do you want to ride with us?' asked
Jo-Ann.

'OK,' Lauren agreed. She and Twilight
set off after the others. He was smaller
than the other two ponies but he kept up
well, twisting and turning and cantering
sure-footedly down the banks. Jo-Ann
was a very daring rider. After cantering
up and down the hills, she started to
jump any bushes or fallen logs she could
find – even logs that had spiky branches

sticking up and that were lying on uneven ground. She didn't seem to worry about safety. Lauren and Grace stopped to watch her.

Lauren gasped as Beauty only just managed to clear a huge tree trunk.

'That was close!' Jo-Ann grinned, pulling Beauty up and patting her. She looked around. 'What shall I do next?' Her eyes fell on the very steep bank. 'I know! How about I try that bank over there?'

'No way!' Grace said. 'It's much too steep and it might be slippery.'

'I bet Beauty could manage it,' Jo-Ann said thoughtfully.

'Don't do it,' Grace advised. 'These

guys have done enough.' She patted
Windfall's warm neck. 'Come on, let's
take them home.'

'I guess they are quite hot,' Jo-Ann
agreed reluctantly. 'Let's walk back to cool
them off.' She turned to Lauren. 'Nice to
meet you, Lauren. See you around.'

'Yeah, bye!' Lauren called.

She waved as the older girls rode off,
and then stroked Twilight's mane. 'Come
on, let's go home too.' She didn't want to
tire him out again. She was looking
forward to flying that night!

As they reached the farm, Lauren saw
Max and Buddy heading out along the
drive. Max had his skateboard with him.

'Are you going round to Leo and
Steven's?' she asked.

Max nodded. 'Yeah, Leo's got a new
skateboard and he said I could try it, then
we're going to take Buddy for a walk.'

Buddy wagged his plumy tail and
woofed. He might not be able to
understand humans in the way that
Twilight could but he could certainly
understand the words *Buddy* and *walk*!

'You'll like that, won't you, boy?' Max
said, giving Buddy a hug. 'You like Leo
and Steven.' Buddy licked his face in
reply and Max giggled.

Lauren grinned. It was great seeing
Max and Buddy so happy together. When
Max had first made friends with their

neighbours, Steven and Leo Vance, he had
neglected Buddy a bit, but then he had
found out his new friends liked dogs as
much as he did and now Buddy always
went with him when he went to their
house.

'See you later, Lauren,' Max said, setting
off again.

'Later,' Lauren replied and she rode
Twilight back to his stable.

After she had untacked him and

washed him down, she turned him out into the field. 'I'll come out this evening and we can go flying. OK?'

Twilight didn't respond.

'Twilight?' Lauren said.

He whickered quietly. *Tonight*, Lauren thought and, giving him a hug, she went in for lunch.

That night, Twilight was waiting for Lauren by the gate. He seemed tense again; he was pacing up and down and his head was held high. Lauren quickly turned him into a unicorn. 'Hi, boy. Are you ready to go flying then?'

Twilight shook his head.

'Why not?' Lauren demanded. 'We

didn't do that much today!'

Twilight interrupted her. 'It's not because I'm tired.'

'So, why can't we go flying then?'

Twilight pawed the ground unhappily. 'Because . . . because I can't.'

Lauren didn't understand. 'What do you mean, you can't?' She touched his neck in concern. 'Are you ill or something?'

'No. I can't go flying because . . .' Twilight took a deep breath and looked miserably at her. 'Because my magic powers have stopped working!'

CHAPTER
Three

Lauren stared. 'What do you mean, your powers have stopped working? For how long?'

Twilight looked at the ground. 'Forever.'

Lauren felt as if a bucket of ice had just been tipped all over her. 'Forever!' she echoed.

Twilight nodded. 'It happens

sometimes,' he said, not meeting her
eyes. 'Unicorns lose their powers.
Their magic just fades and goes away.
It means I can't do any magic any more
– I can't look into the seeing stones; I
can't heal wounds; I can't make people
feel braver. I can't do any of those
things.'

Lauren's mind seemed to spin. 'And
you can't fly?'

'No.'

Lauren was struck by an awful thought.
'But you'll always be able to turn into a
unicorn, won't you? I'll always be able to
speak to you like this?'

'I don't know.' Twilight hesitated.
'Probably not,' he added in a very small

voice. 'My powers will probably all
disappear in the end.'

Lauren's stomach plunged. She didn't
know what to say.

'I . . . I suppose this means you won't
love me any more,' Twilight said.

'What?' Lauren frowned. 'Of course I'll
love you.'

Twilight looked taken aback. 'But . . .
but I won't be able to do magic. I'll just
be an ordinary pony.'

'As if that matters!' Lauren burst out. She was astonished that he could think this would change the way she felt about him. 'Twilight, you're my best friend.' She hugged him fiercely. 'How *could* you think that losing your powers would change that? I loved you before I knew you were a unicorn, remember? It doesn't matter to me whether you're magical or not.'

'So, you won't want me to go away?' Twilight spoke very slowly. 'You won't want to get rid of me?'

'Get rid of you? No way!'

A look of confusion crossed Twilight's face. 'But . . . but I thought . . .' He looked even more upset than before.

'I can't believe you'd think that I'd

want to get rid of you!' Lauren exclaimed. 'All that matters, Twilight, is that we're together.'

Twilight scraped his foot on the ground. 'Oh,' he said in a very small voice.

Feeling utterly bewildered, Lauren put her arms round him. What was going on? A hard lump of tears blocked her throat. But she tried not to cry. Twilight was obviously very upset. She'd only make him more miserable if she started crying.

'Maybe I'd better turn you back into a pony,' she said, her voice coming out in a whisper.

Twilight nodded sadly.

Lauren said the words of the Undoing Spell and Twilight turned back into a pony.

''Night, Twilight,' she whispered.

He whickered unhappily as she walked slowly back to the house.

When she got back to her bedroom, she sat down on the bed. Twilight's magic was fading! She undressed and got into bed. She couldn't believe it. No more magic. No more flying. And, maybe soon, no more talking to her best friend. But the worst thing of all was how unhappy this was making Twilight. Did he really think she wouldn't love him any more, just because he wasn't a unicorn?

★

Lauren lay awake for ages that night and when she woke up, her first thought was that she'd had a bad dream. She blinked, and realized it hadn't been a dream at all. It was real. Twilight was losing his magic powers.

She pulled on her clothes and went downstairs. Her mum, dad and Max were in the kitchen.

'Morning, sleepyhead!' her dad teased.

Not wanting her parents to see how tired she felt in case they wanted to know why, Lauren forced a smile. 'Morning.'

Mrs Foster was making a pot of coffee. 'We almost sent Buddy in to wake you up. Twilight will be wondering where his breakfast is.'

'I'll go and feed him now,' Lauren said, glad of an excuse to get out of the house.

Buddy trotted over to her and pushed his body between her legs. Lauren made a fuss of him to try and hide her sadness from her family. When she sat down to pull her boots on, Buddy plonked his head on her lap and looked up at her with big brown eyes. It was as if he could sense there was something wrong.

'Good boy,' Lauren whispered, blinking hard.

'What time are you going over to Leo and Steven's, Max?' Mrs Foster asked.

Max scraped the last of his cereal bowl clean. 'Half past nine. I can't wait! They got their new puppy last night.'

Lauren had forgotten that Steven and Leo were getting their new puppy that weekend.

'Have they decided what they're going to call her?' asked Mrs Foster.

Max grinned. 'Buggy!'

'Buggy?' Mrs Foster echoed doubtfully.

'It's short for Love Bug; that's what Steven and Leo's mum said the puppy's proper name is.'

Mr Foster shook his head. 'Buddy and Buggy. That's going to be a bit confusing!'

'I think Buggy's a cool name. She and Buddy are going to be best friends!' Max said happily. 'I can't wait to see her.'

Mrs Foster smiled. 'I'm with you there. In fact, I think I might just have to walk round with you when you go to their house this morning.' She glanced at Lauren. 'Do you want to come too, Lauren?'

Knowing that her mum would think it was strange if she said no, Lauren nodded. 'Yes, please.' She stood up and went to the door. First she had to feed Twilight. As she walked down to his

field, she felt odd. She wasn't quite sure
how to act. What would she say to
him?

Twilight was standing by the gate
looking very miserable. His head was low
and his eyes seemed to have lost their
sparkle.

'Hey, boy,' Lauren said.

He nuzzled her gently. Neither of them
met the other's eyes.

Lauren fetched Twilight his breakfast
but he hardly touched it. He nibbled a
few flakes of the coarse mix and then left
the rest.

Lauren stroked him. 'Not feeling
hungry today?'

Twilight shook his head.

'Me neither,' Lauren told him. Just looking at how sad Twilight was made her eyes prickle with tears.

But he'll still be my pony, she reminded herself. *I'll still be able to see him and ride him every day. And the more fuss I make of him, the more he might believe that I do still love him.*

Feeling a bit better, she started on the stable chores – cleaning out and refilling Twilight's water buckets, brushing the concrete in front of the stables and tidying the tack room. After a while, she heard her mum calling.

'Lauren! We're going to Steven and Leo's now!'

'Coming!' Lauren called back.

She went over to where Twilight was standing unhappily by the gate and rubbed his neck. 'I'll be back soon,' she promised, giving him a kiss.

Buggy was the cutest puppy ever! She was a flat-coated retriever with a soft, jet-black coat, bright sparkling eyes, big paws and a tail that never seemed to stop wagging. As Lauren and Max and Mrs Foster crowded round, the puppy wriggled in Leo's arms, trying to lick everyone's faces and hands with her pink tongue. Buddy pressed forward and Buggy licked him on the nose.

'Can I put her on the grass, Mum?' Leo begged.

'Yeah,' Steven said. 'Let's see how she likes Buddy.'

Their mum, Helen, nodded. 'All right.'

As soon as Buggy was on the floor, she bounded over to Buddy, her tail going round and round like a propeller. She was only as high as his tummy but she didn't seem scared at all. She leapt on Buddy, licking his mouth and pulling at his ears.

Buddy's tail started to wag and he crouched down to look at her more closely.

The puppy yapped at him and he woofed back in a deep voice. Then he lay down and let her jump all over him, rolling over on his back so she could scrabble on to his tummy.

After a few minutes they jumped up

and began to chase each other around the garden.

'Looks like they're going to be friends,' Helen smiled.

Leo turned to Max. 'When Buggy gets bigger we'll be able to take them on walks together.'

'And she can run round the skateboard course like Buddy does,' said Steven.

'We can have races!' Leo added.

Max nodded eagerly. 'It'll be cool!'

Lauren smiled. Max was going to have loads of fun taking Buddy to play with Leo, Steven and Buggy. She knew that having friends with pets was great fun. She loved riding with Mel and Jessica.

And I'll still be able to do that when Twilight's magic is gone, she reflected. She thought of Twilight's sad face that morning and suddenly wanted to get back to him. She had to make him realize that it didn't matter if he lost his magic.

'Is it OK if I go back now, Mum?' she asked.

'Of course,' replied Mrs Foster. 'I'll see you later.'

Lauren hurried home. Twilight was standing by the gate where she had left him, not looking any happier. Climbing over it, Lauren put an arm round his neck and leant her cheek against his neck. 'Oh, Twilight,' she whispered. 'Losing your powers must be horrible for you but it's going to be OK, I promise. We'll still be able to have lots of fun together.'

She'd hoped her words might cheer Twilight up but he still looked miserable.

Lauren wracked her brains to think of something she could do to make him feel better. Maybe if they went out for a ride in the woods it would help him realize how much fun they could have, even if he was just a pony.

'How about we go for a ride?' she suggested. 'We could go to the place with the banks and hills again.'

Twilight gave a tiny nod.

Lauren kissed him. 'OK. I'll go and ring Mel and Jessica and see if they want to come too.'

CHAPTER

Four

J essica couldn't come out for a
ride because she was going into
town with her stepsister, Samantha,
but Mel was keen to go to the
woods again.

She came over at eleven. 'So, did you go
to the clearing yesterday?' she asked as they
rode down the track, away from the farm.

'Yes,' Lauren replied. 'There were two

girls there. They let me ride with them.'
She patted Twilight. 'We had fun, didn't
we, boy?' He snorted quietly. Lauren
crossed her fingers. She desperately
wanted him to see what a good time
they could have without magic.

As they reached the clearing they heard
voices.

'That might be those girls,' Lauren said.

She and Mel rode into the clearing.
Sure enough, Jo-Ann and Grace were
there on Beauty and Windfall. They had
set up jumps at the bottom of some of
the banks.

'Hi, Lauren!' Jo-Ann called, waving.
She looked again. 'Mel!' she exclaimed.
'Hello.'

'Hi, Jo-Ann,' Mel called.

'Do you two know each other?' Lauren asked in surprise.

Mel nodded as Jo-Ann rode over to them. 'Our mums are friends,' she explained. She smiled at Jo-Ann. 'Is this your new pony? Mum told me you'd just got one.'

'Yes, this is Beauty,' Jo-Ann replied. The pretty bay tossed her head. 'She's brilliant.

She's really fast and loves jumping. Is
Shadow still jumping OK?'

Mel nodded. 'Ever since last summer
he's been fine.'

Lauren stroked Twilight's neck to hide a
smile. When she had first met Mel,
Shadow had been scared of jumping but
she and Twilight had helped him get over
his fear. It had been one of the first things
they had done together after Lauren had

found out Twilight was a unicorn. He
had been able to use his magic powers to
fill Shadow with courage – enough to
leap out of his barn when it was on fire!
She wondered if he was remembering it
too.

*I suppose we won't be helping any more
people now.* Lauren pushed the thought
away. This wasn't the time to feel sorry
for herself. Twilight needed her to be
cheerful.

'Can we have a go at the jumps?' she
asked Jo-Ann.

'Sure,' Jo-Ann replied.

'Come on!' Grace called.

Soon, Lauren and Mel were cantering
down the banks and over the jumps with

the two older girls. Mel only did the lower jumps but Lauren tried some of the bigger ones. Not all of them, though. Jo-Ann had made a few massive jumps out of logs and old branches.

'I don't know how you dare do that!' Mel called as Jo-Ann rode down a particularly steep bank with a huge brush jump at the bottom.

'It's fun!' Jo-Ann laughed, pulling Beauty to a halt. The pony snorted and pulled at her bit.

'Why don't you have a go?' Jo-Ann urged Lauren and Mel.

Mel shook her head. 'It's way too big for Shadow and me.'

Jo-Ann turned to Lauren. 'How about

you, Lauren? Twilight seems really good at jumping.'

Lauren hesitated. Part of her longed to canter down the bank and fly over the jump, but then she looked at the steep uneven surface and shook her head. Jo-Ann might have managed it fine but it did look tricky. She'd never forgive herself if Twilight hurt himself. 'No, I don't think I will,' she said.

Jo-Ann looked teasingly at her. 'Chicken!'

'Jo-Ann!' Grace protested. 'Don't hassle Lauren. If she doesn't want to do it, she doesn't have to.'

'Sorry.' Jo-Ann shrugged. 'Looks like I'll have to do it on my own, then.' She

cantered towards the bank and sped
down it. Beauty cleared the jump easily.

Jo-Ann patted her and headed towards
the really steep bank that no one had
dared to go down yet.

'Be careful, Jo!' Grace warned.

'Stop fussing,' Jo-Ann replied. 'Beauty
will manage it fine.'

The other three watched as she headed
towards it. Beauty sped up, fighting for
her head. Jo-Ann circled her, got her
steady and then tried again. It was so
steep that Beauty had to tuck her hocks
right underneath her. Lauren gasped as
the bank crumbled a little and Beauty slid
a few metres, but Jo-Ann sat very still and
let her find her footing again. In a couple

more strides, they safely reached the
bottom of the bank.

'Good girl!' Jo-Ann praised.

'Cool!' Mel said.

Grace nodded. 'That was great riding,
Jo.'

'She's a great pony!' Jo-Ann said,
patting the mare. She looked at the bank.
'Maybe I could put a jump at the
bottom.'

Grace shook her head. 'It's hard enough
to get down without a jump there.'

'I suppose,' Jo-Ann replied, not
sounding convinced.

'Come on,' Grace said. 'Why don't we
take the ponies to the creek for a drink?'

'All right.' Jo-Ann turned to Lauren
and Mel. 'Are you going to come as well?'

They nodded and the four of them set
off through the trees. As they rode,
Lauren learned that Grace and Jo-Ann
kept their ponies at a livery stables that
Grace's mum owned. It was fun hearing
about the ponies there, and about all the
shows that Grace and Jo-Ann competed
in. Lauren hoped Twilight was enjoying
himself too.

It doesn't matter one bit that he can't be a unicorn, she told herself. *We'll still be able to go for rides like this and do all sorts of things. After all, Mel and Jessica love Shadow and Sandy and they aren't unicorns.*

Lauren frowned as she realized she'd been so shocked by the news the night before that she hadn't asked Twilight why unicorns lost their powers at all, or if there was any way of stopping it. Perhaps there was some way of getting his powers back! Hope flickered through her. If there was anything – anything at all – she could do, then she would give it a try to make him happy again.

I'll ask him tonight, she thought. Then another idea struck her. What about her unicorn book? It had lots of information about unicorns in it. Maybe one of the chapters would explain how they could stop Twilight's magic from fading.

I'll look at it when I get home, she decided.

As soon as Lauren untacked Twilight after their ride, she ran into the house and found her precious book. *The Life of a Unicorn* was a very old book with a faded blue cover. Mrs Fontana, who owned the bookshop in town, had given it to Lauren when she had first got Twilight. Mrs Fontana was one of the few people who knew about Twilight, because she had once owned a unicorn herself.

Lauren began to leaf through the yellowing pages. There were chapters on unicorn myths, unicorn habits, and all sorts of information about Arcadia, the magic land that the unicorns came from.

Lauren flicked through chapter after chapter. There had to be something about unicorns losing their powers!

She stopped at the end of the book. There was nothing. Not a single mention of a unicorn's magic fading.

Weird, Lauren thought. *Twilight made it sound like it happened quite often. It's odd the book doesn't say anything about it at all.*

She frowned. She'd have to question him more that night.

*

'Twilight, I looked in the unicorn book and it didn't say anything about unicorns losing their powers,' Lauren said as soon as she had turned Twilight into a unicorn.

'Well, it does happen,' Twilight said quickly.

'Is there anything that can be done to stop it or to bring them back?' Lauren asked.

'No,' he muttered, scraping at the ground with his front hoof. 'I don't think so.'

'Maybe if you tell me everything you know about it, we can think of something to try,' Lauren urged him.

Twilight looked uncomfortable. 'I can't remember much.'

Lauren frowned. 'How can we find out more?' Her eyes widened. 'Of course!' she exclaimed. 'Mrs Fontana! She knows lots about unicorns – we can ask her.'

Twilight shook his head. 'I'm sure she won't be able to help, Lauren . . .'

But Lauren refused to give up hope. 'It's worth asking her,' she interrupted. Mrs Fontana always seemed to know what to do when there was a problem with Twilight. 'I'll see if Mum will drive me to her shop in the morning.' She hugged Twilight. 'Don't worry, Mrs Fontana will be able to help us, I'm sure!'

Twilight snorted unhappily. Lauren couldn't understand why he didn't look convinced. After all, if he was so depressed about losing his magic powers, surely he'd try anything to get them back?

Five

Deep in the heart of Arcadia, the three Unicorn Elders stood by the stone table, their golden, silver and bronze horns sparkling in the moonlight. The picture that had been there moments before had vanished and all that was left of the magic was a wisp of purple smoke drifting across the table.

'Twilight is very unhappy,' Ira, the

unicorn with the golden horn, said heavily.

'He is so young,' sighed Rohan, the bronze-horned unicorn. 'And he loves Lauren very much.'

Sidra lifted her head, her silver horn flashing in the starlight. 'Yes, but this is how it has to be.' She pricked up her ears. 'He must see that this is for the best - that it is an honour to be chosen. Maybe I should visit him again and talk to him some more.'

'Yes,' the other two unicorns agreed.

'Will you go tomorrow night?' Ira asked.

Sidra nodded. 'I will.'

★

'Is there something in particular you want from the bookshop?' Mrs Foster asked as she drove Lauren into town the next morning. It was a very cold day and the sky was turning a snowy white.

'I just want a new book to read,' Lauren replied casually. 'I've got the money that Auntie Hilary sent to me, and I thought I might spend it on a book.'

Mrs Foster nodded. 'Any idea what book you'd like?'

'Not yet,' Lauren said. 'Is it OK if I spend some time browsing?'

'Well, it looks like it's going to snow, so we'd better not be too long,' her mum replied. 'I'll leave you at Mrs Fontana's while I do the rest of my shopping.'

'Thanks,' Lauren said, feeling relieved. Hopefully she'd get to spend some time with Mrs Fontana on her own. She stared out of the window at the houses flashing by and, as soft snowflakes began to fall, she wondered what Mrs Fontana would say.

Mrs Fontana's bookshop never seemed to change. There were always piles of books on the floor and the air always smelt slightly of blackcurrants. Lauren thought it was the smell of magic even though her mum said it was the fruit tea that Mrs Fontana drank. The elderly lady was standing at the counter with her grey hair tied back in a bun and her soft yellow shawl wrapped round her shoulders. She was talking to Walter,

her little black and white terrier dog.

'Hello, Lauren,' she said, looking up as Lauren entered. 'How are you?'

'Fine, thank you,' Lauren replied. She glanced around to check that there was no one else in the shop.

'We're alone,' Mrs Fontana said, as if she could read Lauren's thoughts. She frowned. 'Are you all right, my dear? You look worried.'

The words burst out of Lauren. 'Oh, Mrs Fontana, I really need your help. Twilight's losing his magic powers!'

Mrs Fontana looked astonished. 'What?'

Lauren quickly told her everything. 'He said that it happens to unicorns

sometimes but I can't find any mention
of it in the book and I want to know if
there's anything we can do. It's making
him so unhappy!' She looked pleadingly
at Mrs Fontana. 'Do you know if there's
anything that will stop his magic from
fading?'

Mrs Fontana looked puzzled. 'I'm sorry,
Lauren, but I don't know what to say. I've
never heard of a unicorn losing its
powers before – not permanently, anyway.
Are you sure that's what Twilight said was
happening?'

'Positive,' Lauren replied. 'He said it
often happens and that there's nothing we
can do.'

'How strange.' Mrs Fontana rubbed her

forehead. 'Why don't you tell me exactly what happened?'

Lauren sat on a long-legged stool and rested her chin on her hands. 'He was fine one day, and the next he seemed really miserable. At first he said he was just tired but then he told me about his magic fading. He's so unhappy! I've tried telling him that I'll still love him even if he's just a regular pony but it doesn't seem to have helped.' She bit her lip. 'It's awful seeing him like this, Mrs Fontana! If there's anything I can do, I want to do it.'

'I'm sure you do, Lauren.' Mrs Fontana hesitated. 'But you know, I think there's something else going on and Twilight's not telling you everything. Unicorns

don't lose their powers permanently. It
just doesn't happen.'

Lauren's heart leapt. 'Really?'

Mrs Fontana nodded.

'So why have Twilight's powers gone?'
Lauren asked. 'Why can't he fly any
more?'

'I don't know,' Mrs Fontana admitted. 'I
can only assume that there's something
Twilight hasn't told you about. My advice
is to try and get him to talk to you. But
don't push him too hard,' she warned. 'He
might clam up even more.'

'OK,' Lauren agreed. Her head was
whirling. It felt odd to think that there
was something Twilight wasn't telling
her. 'I just don't understand why he

would keep something secret. I'm his
best friend – he should be able to tell me
anything!'

'Oh, Lauren, people keep secrets for all
sorts of reasons,' Mrs Fontana replied.
'Twilight is probably doing what he
thinks is best. Just let him know that
you'll listen when he's ready to talk.' She
squeezed Lauren's hand. 'He might be
your unicorn, Lauren, but he's also your
friend. Treat him like you would any of
your other friends if you thought they
had a problem. He'll tell you what's going
on in his own good time.'

Just then the doorbell tinkled and a
man came in with a little boy. Walter
trotted over to say hello, and Lauren

knew her conversation with Mrs Fontana
was over.

'Thanks, Mrs Fontana,' she said.

'Good luck!' Mrs Fontana smiled. 'And
now, you'd better choose a book before
your mum gets back and wonders what
you've been doing all this time.'

Lauren thought about what Mrs Fontana
had said all day. She felt better knowing
that Mrs Fontana had never heard of a
unicorn's magic fading away permanently
before. She just wished she knew exactly
what was going on.

'Are you sure there's nothing else you
want to tell me?' Lauren said to Twilight
as she stroked his silky mane that night.

'No,' he sighed.

'Really sure?' Lauren persisted.

'Yes. Can we talk about something else?'

Lauren bit her lip with frustration. She remembered what Mrs Fontana had said about letting Twilight talk to her in his own time, so she just nodded. 'Sure. But you can tell me anything, Twilight, you know that. Anything at all.'

He stared miserably at the ground. Lauren couldn't bear seeing him look so sad.

'I know, how about I go and get you some carrots from the tack room as a treat? Dad put a new sack in there this afternoon.'

Twilight nodded and she hurried away.

When she came back with the carrots, Twilight was shaking his head. 'I've got to tell her!' he was muttering. 'I can't do this.'

Lauren froze. What was he talking about?

'I just can't!' Twilight said to himself.

'Twilight?' Lauren whispered.

Twilight looked round, startled. 'Lauren! I didn't see you there.'

'What were you talking about?' she asked, hurrying over. 'What have you got to tell me?'

'Nothing. I . . . I wasn't talking about you,' Twilight said quickly.

Lauren felt her temper flare. She knew

that wasn't true. 'Twilight!' she exclaimed
angrily. 'Just . . .' She broke off, recalling
what Mrs Fontana had said about not
putting pressure on him in case he
clammed up even more. 'OK,' she said,
trying to stay calm. 'If you don't want to
talk about it, that's fine.'

Twilight relaxed slightly and as she fed
him a carrot, she changed the subject. 'It
was fun yesterday, wasn't it? Riding with
Jo-Ann and Grace, I mean. Do you like
Beauty and Windfall?'

Twilight nodded. 'Yes, and I liked
cantering up and down the banks too.'

'We'll have to go again,' Lauren said.
'And go on some more fun rides and
wander by the creek. There are so many

things we can do, especially when
summer comes,' she went on, trying to
remind him that they could have fun
whether he was a unicorn or not. 'Maybe
we could even go camping!'

'Maybe,' Twilight said in a quiet voice.

Lauren stayed with him for an hour,
talking about all the great things they
could do together, before she went inside.
She sat down on her bed, feeling
frustrated. However nice it was talking to
Twilight, she still hadn't found out what
was going on.

Getting undressed, she climbed into
bed and pulled her duvet over her. But
she couldn't sleep. She and Twilight were
best friends. They shouldn't keep secrets

from each other. *I wouldn't keep a secret
from him*, she thought.

She hesitated and then pushed her
duvet back. She couldn't go on like this.
Mrs Fontana might have said to take it
gently but she *had* to know what was
going on. Getting out of bed, she pulled
her clothes back on. Then she crept
downstairs and hurried outside. She
would beg Twilight to tell her what the
matter was, make him see that whatever
it was, they could overcome it together.

Feeling fired up with determination, she ran down the path to his field. Suddenly she stopped dead.

'Twilight!' she whispered in astonishment.

Twilight was standing in his field, but he wasn't a pony, like she had left him. His coat was gleaming silvery-white and his horn was glittering. He was a unicorn!

And that wasn't all. Standing beside him was another unicorn! It had its head bent and was talking urgently to Twilight. Lauren stared in shock. This unicorn was bigger than Twilight, with a coat that sparkled like freshly fallen snow. It had a long silver horn, glittering dark eyes and

a face so beautiful that just looking at it
made Lauren hold her breath.

The unicorn whinnied and flew into
the air without noticing Lauren.

Stunned, Lauren watched Twilight
plunge upwards too, and side by side the
two unicorns cantered away into the
starry sky.

CHAPTER
Six

Lauren took a step forward and stared at the empty sky. Twilight had said he couldn't fly any more. He had told her that his powers had gone. How *could* he have just flown away?

There was only one answer. Twilight had been lying to her!

Lauren shook her head in disbelief. She couldn't believe that all the time, when

she'd been so worried about him, he
hadn't lost his powers at all.

Turning, she ran back to the house.

When she reached her bedroom she
threw herself down on her bed. The
unicorn book slipped on to the floor and
landed with a thud. It fell awkwardly, half
open, with its beautiful old pages bent
and creased. Lauren automatically reached
down to pick it up. As she did, she
noticed that it had fallen open at a
picture. Icy fingers ran down her spine. It
showed two unicorns cantering into the
sky – one big, one small, exactly like
Twilight and the unicorn she'd seen just
now.

With her heart thudding painfully,

Lauren pulled the book closer and read
the title below the picture:

> *A Unicorn Elder taking a Chosen*
> *Unicorn back to Arcadia.*

Not understanding, Lauren scanned the
rest of the words.

> *Pony unicorns who prove themselves to be*

particularly brave and resourceful in the human world will often be chosen to return to Arcadia. There they will train to be assistants to the Unicorn Elders, helping the Elders to rule Arcadia and watch over the human world. It is a great honour to be chosen and, in time, these chosen unicorns will one day become Unicorn Elders themselves. A chosen unicorn will be visited by a Unicorn Elder several times before the unicorn has to say goodbye to his or her human friend and leave the human world forever.

Leave the human world forever. The words echoed around in Lauren's head. Twilight must have been chosen to go to Arcadia! Was that where he'd been going with the other unicorn tonight?

Did that mean she was never going to see him again?

Jumping off her bed, Lauren raced to her window.

Twilight was in his field, grazing peacefully. For one wild moment Lauren wondered if she'd just imagined the sight of him flying into the sky with another unicorn. Maybe it was all a dream? But it wasn't. She'd seen both unicorns flying away as clearly as she saw Twilight in his field now.

She sank down on to the window seat. The Unicorn Elder must have been visiting Twilight that night. But maybe the *next* time . . .

'No,' Lauren whispered out loud. 'He can't go to Arcadia.'

But the more she thought about it, the more it all made sense. That first morning when he'd been so quiet – well, that must have been after the first visit from the Unicorn Elder, after Twilight had been told he'd been chosen. And the reason he had looked so sad even when Lauren had said she didn't mind if he lost his powers must have been because he'd known that they wouldn't be together much longer.

Why didn't he tell me? Lauren thought desperately. *He must have known he was going to have to tell me some time. Unless . . .*

Her stomach flipped over.

Perhaps Twilight hadn't been planning to tell her at all. Perhaps he'd been intending just to vanish one night.

Twilight wouldn't do that, she told herself, but why else would Twilight have kept his news secret? Why else would he have lied to her?

Lauren began to tremble. Moving like a robot, she took off her clothes and pulled on her pyjamas, then crawled under the duvet. She couldn't stop shivering. She felt utterly betrayed by her best friend. How could he have thought of leaving without telling her? How could he have thought of leaving at all?

Oh, Twilight, she cried silently in her head. *I could never leave you.*

Pulling the duvet over her head, a sob choked through her and soon her pillow was soaked with tears.

The next morning, Lauren stayed in bed until she heard her mum getting up. For the first time ever, she didn't want to go out to Twilight's field. But when she heard her mum waking Max up, she knew she couldn't stay in bed much longer. She had to get up now to avoid facing her mum and Max in the kitchen. They would see at once that she'd been crying. Putting on her crumpled jeans, she hurried outside before they came downstairs.

Twilight was waiting by his gate. To Lauren's surprise, he lifted his head and

whinnied happily. When she reached the
gate he nuzzled her as if they were best
friends again.

Her heart sank with misery. She knew
why he was happy this morning. It was
because he'd spent the night before
talking to the other unicorn, and
planning his return to Arcadia.

She pushed him away. 'I'll get your
breakfast,' she said, barely able to stop her
voice shaking with hurt. Ignoring his
look of surprise, she walked away.

When she returned with his coarse
mix, Twilight whinnied.

'Here,' she said abruptly, putting the
bucket down.

Twilight nudged her but she stepped

back. 'No, don't do that!' she exclaimed.

Twilight took a mouthful and then, looking at her cheekily from under his forelock, he snorted the food into the air. Normally when he messed around, it made Lauren smile. But right then, her heart felt like a stone in her chest. How could he be so cheerful when he knew he was leaving her forever?

She guessed that whatever the other
unicorn had said to him the night before
had made Twilight realize that his
decision to leave was the right one.

Her throat ached. Turning round, she
hurried away before he could see the
tears in her eyes.

Twilight whickered but she ignored him
and carried on. She forced herself not to
turn round even though he whinnied
again and again. He was still whinnying
when she reached the house and went
inside, slamming the door behind her.

After breakfast, Lauren went to her room.
To avoid going outside she decided to
tidy her room. She had just taken all the

books off the shelves above her bed when
Mel rang.

'Hi!' Mel said cheerfully. 'Shall we go
for a ride today? There isn't much snow –
we could go to the clearing again.'

'Um . . . no thanks.' Lauren didn't feel
like doing anything with Twilight.

'Why not?' Mel said in surprise.

'I don't feel very well,' Lauren lied.

'What's the matter?' asked Mel.

Lauren thought quickly. 'I've got a
cold. My throat's really sore. I'd better not
talk for long.'

'Oh, OK. Well, I hope you feel better
soon,' Mel told her. 'I'll give you a ring
tonight. Maybe we could go for a ride
tomorrow?'

'Maybe,' Lauren whispered. Saying goodbye, she put the phone down.

She walked over to the window and stared out. Twilight was standing by the gate with his ears pricked up hopefully. He looked like he was waiting for her. How could he not realize how much he was hurting her?

Wrapping her arms round herself, Lauren tried to imagine life without him. No unicorn, no pony, no best friend.

As if sensing that she was watching, Twilight looked up at the window. Swallowing her tears, Lauren quickly turned away.

CHAPTER

Seven

As Lauren fed Twilight that evening and refilled his water buckets, he nudged her again and again. Lauren guessed he was trying to tell her that he wanted to be turned into a unicorn.

'I'm not going to come out later,' she muttered. 'I'll see you in the morning, Twilight.' *If you're still here.*

Twilight whickered urgently but

Lauren shook her head.

Her heart aching, she trudged back to the house.

She was just pulling her boots off when the phone rang. It was Jessica. 'Hi. How are you feeling?'

'Fine,' Lauren said, before remembering she was supposed to be ill. 'My throat's still a bit sore though,' she added hastily.

'Mel said you weren't well. She's here now – she's staying the night.'

'Hi, Lauren!' Lauren heard Mel shout in the background.

'Are you going to be OK to ride tomorrow?' Jessica asked.

'I'm not sure,' Lauren said. 'I don't think so.'

'Is everything all right?' said Jessica.
'You sound really down.'

'I'm OK,' Lauren told her.

Mel took the phone from Jessica. 'Are
you still feeling ill?'

'Yes.' Lauren quickly changed the
subject. 'How was the ride today?'

'Fun,' Mel answered. 'We went to the
clearing again after lunch. Jo-Ann and
Grace weren't there this time.'

Lauren could hear Twilight
whinnying but she ignored him.
'Jo-Ann had a riding lesson
today and was going to go
to the clearing later this
afternoon,' Lauren
remembered.

'Yes, that's right,' said
Mel. 'She must have got
there after us. I wonder if
she tried that bank again.
She's so brave!'

'Yeah,' Lauren said.

'Well, I'd better go,' Mel told her. 'I'll
ring you tomorrow. Get better soon!
Jess and I want to go on as many rides
as we can before it gets really snowy but

we don't want to go without you.'

Lauren hung up the phone and sat down. When Twilight left she wouldn't be able to go riding with Mel and Jessica any more. Slowly, her unhappiness turned to anger. *I'll get another pony*, she thought. *I don't need Twilight. I don't need him at all.*

She stood up and started laying the table for supper. Max was staying at Steven and Leo's house that night so it was just her and her mum and dad. She had just finished setting three places when the phone rang again.

Lauren picked it up. 'Granger's Farm, Lauren Foster speaking.'

'Oh hello, Lauren. It's Mrs Cassidy.'

'Hi,' said Lauren, wondering why Mel's

mum was ringing her when Mel was
staying at Jessica's house.

'Is your mum there?'

'Yes, I think she's in her study. I'll just
get her.' Lauren carried the phone
through to her mum's study. 'Mrs
Cassidy's on the phone!'

Her mum took the receiver. 'Hi.'
Lauren was about to leave the room
when she heard her mum's voice
change. 'Really?' Mrs Foster sounded
alarmed. 'The pony came back on her
own?'

Lauren frowned. *Pony? What pony?*

'Of course we'll help,' her mum was
saying. 'I'll get Tim and we'll come right
over.'

'What was that about?' Lauren asked as
her mum put the phone down.

'A friend of the Cassidys went riding
in the woods this afternoon, and her
pony came back without her half an hour
ago. The pony seems fine but the girl
hasn't been seen since. Her mum's
organizing a search party.'

'What is the girl's name?' Lauren said,
her heart beating faster.

'Jo-Ann,' Mrs Foster replied, heading through to the kitchen.

'Jo-Ann!' Lauren echoed.

'Do you know her?' Mrs Foster asked.

'I've met her in the woods a few times.' Lauren dug her nails into her palms. Jo-Ann was in trouble!

'Well, hopefully we'll find her soon,' said Mrs Foster, peering doubtfully through the window. It was already getting dark and it had started to snow again. 'I'm going to get your dad and head over to the Cassidys' place. Do you want to come?'

Lauren hesitated, thinking fast. 'No,' she said. 'I think I'll stay here.'

'OK. I'll ring you when there's some

news.' Mrs Foster kissed her. 'And try not
to worry, honey. I'm sure we'll find
Jo-Ann.'

Lauren watched her mum getting into
the truck and heading off to the barns.
What should she do?

There was only one answer.

As soon as the truck's headlights
disappeared down the drive, she pulled
on her boots and coat and began to run
down the path to Twilight's field.

'Twilight!' she shouted. 'Twilight!
Quick!'

CHAPTER

Eight

Twilight's whinny reached Lauren
long before she could see him. As
she raced up to the gate, heart pounding,
he trotted over, whickering in delight.

She panted out the words of the
Turning Spell. In a flash, Twilight turned
into a unicorn.

'Lauren, what's the –'

'Listen,' she interrupted him. 'I've only

turned you into a unicorn because I need your help. Jo-Ann's missing. I think she might have fallen off somewhere in the forest and we need to find her. I want you to use your magic to look into a seeing stone and see where she is.'

Twilight started to speak. 'But –'

'Don't tell me you can't do it!' Lauren burst out, her anger and hurt spilling over. 'I *know* you can. I know you've just been lying to me because you don't want to be my unicorn any more!'

Twilight was astounded. 'What?'

'Just do the magic, Twilight!' Lauren
exclaimed furiously. 'Then you can go
back to Arcadia! Yes, I know that's what
you're planning,' she went on. 'I know
you've been visited by a Unicorn Elder
to talk about it, but right now I don't
care.' Tears burned in her eyes. 'Just help
Jo-Ann. Then you can go!'

'But Lauren!' Twilight protested. 'I'm
not going anywhere.'

'Don't lie!' Lauren cried. 'I know it's
true.'

'It's not!' Twilight insisted. 'It's true a
Unicorn Elder did come and ask me to
go to Arcadia. She told me I'd been
chosen to be an assistant to the Elders,

but last night, I saw her again and told her I wouldn't go.' His voice dropped. 'I told her I couldn't leave you, Lauren.'

Lauren stared at him. 'You're . . . you're not going back?' she whispered.

Twilight shook his head. 'The Unicorn Elder told me that if I don't go, I might lose my unicorn powers for real but I

don't care.' He looked at Lauren with his
dark eyes. 'You're right. As long as we're
together, nothing else matters. I'm your
unicorn, Lauren, whether I can do magic
or not.'

Lauren swallowed. 'You lied to me,' she
said in a shaky voice. 'You told me your
powers were going.'

'I'm sorry,' Twilight mumbled, looking wretched. 'I only did it because I couldn't bear to hurt you. I thought that if I said my magic was fading, you wouldn't mind so much when I went away. But now I'm not going anywhere – I've said no!'

Lauren's mind whirled. *He wasn't going. It had all been a mistake . . .*

Twilight nuzzled her hair. 'Look, we can sort this out later. We should be trying to find Jo-Ann now.'

His words jerked Lauren back to reality. 'You're right!' she exclaimed. Jo-Ann needed their help. 'We need a seeing stone.' Taking hold of his mane, she swung herself on to his back.

'Over by the tree!' Twilight said and he

cantered towards the edge of the field. He halted under the large oak tree beside a pinky-grey rock of rose quartz. Twilight bent his head and touched the rock with his horn. 'Help us find Jo-Ann,' he murmured.

There was a burst of purple smoke and the surface of the rock turned into a shimmering mirror. In the mirror, a picture formed of a girl lying in a crumpled heap on a frosty track.

'It's Jo-Ann!' Lauren gasped. 'She's injured! And she must be freezing!' She looked more closely at the picture. 'It's the clearing with the banks!' she said. 'Come on, let's fly there!'

Twilight nodded eagerly. Lauren climbed on to his back and, with a snort, he plunged into the sky.

The wind whipped against Lauren's cheeks as they swooped through the air. She'd been desperate to fly again ever since Twilight told her he was losing his powers, but now she was too worried to enjoy it. Her heart thudded wildly. How badly injured was Jo-Ann? She had been lying so still in the seeing stone. Fear gripped Lauren. 'Faster, Twilight!'

He tossed his head and galloped faster over the trees.

Although the clearing was quite hard to get to along the tracks in the woods,

Twilight got there in no time at all by flying above the treetops. 'There she is!' he cried as they swooped into the clearing.

Jo-Ann was lying at the bottom of the steepest bank, beside a jump made out of branches and logs. Her eyes were closed and her leg was twisted at a strange angle.

'She must have tried that jump!' Lauren gasped.

Twilight landed beside Jo-Ann and Lauren scrambled off his back.

'She's still breathing,' Twilight said in relief.

'Jo-Ann?' Lauren said gently.

The girl didn't move.

Lauren turned to Twilight. 'What do we do?'

'I'll try and help her with my magic.' Twilight bent down until his horn was touching Jo-Ann's leg. Lauren watched as he closed his eyes in concentration. They had used his magic powers before to heal wounds but no one had ever needed it as much as Jo-Ann did now.

Please let this work, Lauren prayed. *Please let Twilight's magic help Jo-Ann.*

CHAPTER

Nine

Twilight's horn shone even brighter. For a moment nothing happened, but then Lauren saw some of the tension leave Jo-Ann's face, and she shifted so that her leg was lying more naturally. Twilight lightly touched his horn against Jo-Ann's forehead. Again it glowed with magic. A few seconds later, Jo-Ann's eyelids fluttered and she sighed.

'The magic needs some time to work,'
Twilight whispered to Lauren. 'Her leg
was broken and she's had a bad bang to
her head, but I think she'll be OK.'

Lauren's knees felt weak with relief.
'We should get her home. Will it be all
right to move her?' She knew it could be
dangerous to move someone who was
badly injured.

Twilight nodded. 'My magic will
protect her.'

'Let's take her to the Cassidys' farm,'
Lauren suggested. 'It's closer, and that's
where the search party was meeting.'

Twilight nodded and knelt down so
that Lauren could lift Jo-Ann on to his
back. She was bigger than Lauren and

because she was unconscious it was hard to get her on to Twilight's back but at last Lauren managed it. Scrambling up beside her, she put her arms round her and Twilight smoothly took off.

As they flew, colour started to return to Jo-Ann's cheeks. Lauren held on to her tightly. *Please let Twilight be right*, she thought, *please let her be OK*.

Suddenly Twilight tensed. 'There are some people ahead. I can hear their voices. I'd better fly round another way. We don't want them to see us.'

Lauren started to nod but then she had a thought. 'It could be part of the search party looking for Jo-Ann. I bet they've come to check the clearing.' She strained

her ears but couldn't hear anything. 'Can you tell who it is, Twilight?'

Hovering in the air, Twilight listened hard. 'I can hear your dad and a few other people. I think one of them's Mrs Cassidy!'

Lauren felt a rush of relief. 'Let's fly down. If I turn you into a pony I can say I rode to the clearing and found Jo-Ann there.'

Twilight nodded and cantered down. As he landed behind some oak trees, Jo-Ann stirred and her eyelids fluttered. Lauren had a feeling that she was turning Twilight back into a pony just in time!

She helped Jo-Ann off Twilight's back

and gently leaned her against the trunk of a tree.

'Where am I?' Jo-Ann murmured, still with her eyes closed.

Lauren quickly whispered the words of the Undoing Spell.

There was a purple flash and Jo-Ann's eyes shot open. 'What was that?' she gasped.

'Nothing,' Lauren said as, behind Jo-Ann, Twilight transformed into a pony.

Jo-Ann blinked and stared at her. 'Lauren? Is that you? Where am I?'

'In the woods,' Lauren replied. 'I think you must have fallen off Beauty and been knocked out. Don't worry, there are people coming. They'll be able to help.'

Twilight whinnied loudly and through
the trees Lauren heard the sound of
voices getting closer. 'We're over here!'
she called.

As Twilight whinnied again, Jo-Ann
gripped Lauren's arm. 'Where's Beauty? Is
she OK?'

'She's at home,' Lauren said. 'She's fine.
She went back to the stables without you.'

Jo-Ann rubbed her eyes. 'I can't
remember anything. I was riding Beauty

and then . . .' she hesitated. 'I can
remember this weird feeling, like I was
flying on a horse through the air.'

Lauren hid a smile. 'You must have
bumped your head pretty hard!'

Jo-Ann laughed weakly. 'Yeah, flying!
As if!'

Just then, the search party arrived.
Lauren's dad was with Mrs Cassidy and
a few other adults that Lauren didn't
know. They looked very relieved indeed

to see Jo-Ann sitting up and talking.

One of them, a woman with short blonde hair, ran forward. 'Jo, honey! Are you OK?'

'I'm fine, Mum,' said Jo-Ann. 'I've just got a terrible headache and my leg hurts a bit. The last thing I remember was being on Beauty. I guess I must have tried to ride too fast down the slope and fallen off. It was a really dumb thing to do. I'm sorry.'

Her mum hugged her hard. 'The most important thing is that you're OK. It's lucky you weren't badly hurt!'

'I'll ring my husband,' said Mrs Cassidy, taking her phone out of her pocket. 'He'll bring the pick-up to take Jo-Ann

home. Then we should let the others
know we've found her.'

Mr Foster hurried over to Lauren.
'What were you doing in the woods?
How did you find Jo-Ann?'

Lauren took a breath. 'Well, after you
and Mum had gone, I realized that Jo-
Ann might be in the clearing we've been
riding in. So I got Twilight and decided
to have a look.' *It's almost the truth*, she
thought. 'I found her lying by the slope,'
she went on. 'I put her on Twilight and
started to bring her home. Then I heard
your voices, so we shouted to you.'

Her dad hugged her. 'Well done.
Though really you shouldn't have gone out
into the woods on your own in the dark.

It would have been best to ring us first.'

'I'm sorry,' Lauren said.

'It's OK.' Her dad smiled. 'It's all worked out fine in the end.'

There was the sound of an engine and headlights appeared through the trees. Jo-Ann's mum and Mrs Cassidy helped Jo-Ann up. 'Time to get you home,' said Mrs Cassidy.

Jo-Ann turned to look at Lauren. 'Thanks for finding me, Lauren.'

Lauren smiled. 'That's OK. See you.'

'Yeah.' Jo-Ann smiled back as her mum helped her towards the truck. She was limping, but her leg wasn't broken like it had been in the clearing. Twilight's magic had worked!

Mr Foster put an arm round Lauren's shoulders. 'Do you want me to walk back with you?'

'It's OK,' she said. 'You go in the truck. I'll ride Twilight. It's not far and I'll get home faster if I can canter.'

Her dad nodded. 'OK. I know you'll be safe with Twilight.' He patted Twilight's neck. 'Best pony in the world, aren't you, fella?'

Twilight snorted.

'See you at home,' Mr Foster smiled.

He hurried to join the others in the truck. As the sound of the engine faded, Lauren turned to Twilight. Now that all the excitement was over, she realized that they had some talking to do. She said the words of the Turning Spell.

In a second, Twilight was a unicorn again.

For a moment neither of them spoke. When they'd been helping Jo-Ann, everything else had been forgotten – all the unhappiness, all the lies, all the worries about what would happen next. But now they were alone again, everything came flooding back.

Lauren cleared her throat. 'So, you're not going back to Arcadia?'

'No.' Twilight took a breath. 'No, I'm not.'

Their eyes met and they both took a step towards each other, speaking at the same time.

'Oh, Twilight, I felt so . . .'

'I'm sorry, Lauren, I never meant . . .'

They both stopped.

'You go first,' Twilight said.

'No, you,' Lauren told him.

He lifted his muzzle to her face. 'I'm sorry,' he breathed. 'I never meant to hurt you. I only lied about my powers going because I thought it would make things easier for you. I love you, Lauren.'

She swallowed. 'I know. I love you too. But I wish you'd told me the truth all along. When I saw you with that other unicorn in the sky, I thought that you'd been lying because you were planning on going back to Arcadia without telling me. It was awful, the worst feeling ever.' She touched his neck. 'It's kind of my fault though. I should have known better. I should have trusted you.'

'I should have told you the truth.' Twilight sighed. 'I just felt so confused. It's a great honour to be asked to go back to Arcadia. I've never heard of a unicorn saying no.'

Lauren looked at him. 'But you did.'

Twilight nodded. 'For you.'

Lauren rested her forehead against his.
She was remembering what he had told
her before. 'Is it true that if you don't go,
you'll lose your magic powers?'

Twilight nodded. 'That's what the Elder
said. But I don't care. So long as I'm with

you, Lauren, I don't mind giving up my magic.'

Lauren bit her lip. She knew how much his magic meant to him. *I can't make him give it up for me*, she thought. *I can't*. No matter how much it hurt, she had to let him go. 'You . . .' Her voice dropped to a whisper. 'You should go.'

Twilight took a step back. 'What?'

Lauren's heart felt like it was breaking. But she couldn't make him give up his magic. 'Twilight, you have to go back,' she said, tears filling her eyes. 'You're brilliant at using your powers. Look how you helped Jo-Ann tonight. If you were in Arcadia you could help so many people. I can't keep you here.'

'But I don't want to leave you, Lauren,' Twilight said desperately.

'You have to.' A sob burst from her. 'We both know you do.'

'No,' Twilight said, shaking his head in dismay.

Just then, there was the sound of a twig snapping behind them. They swung round in alarm.

A Unicorn Elder was standing in the trees at the side of the clearing. She was much bigger than Twilight, and her silver horn glittered in the moonlight.

Lauren stared at the unicorn in horror, a single thought leaping into her head.

She's come to take Twilight away.

CHAPTER

Ten

The Unicorn Elder stepped forward
and bowed her head. 'Hello,
Lauren.'

Lauren couldn't speak. She gripped
Twilight's mane.

'My name is Sidra,' said the unicorn.

Twilight faced the unicorn bravely. 'I
won't go! I won't! I told you –'

'It's all right, Twilight,' Sidra interrupted

him. 'I have not come to take you away.' Her beautiful eyes shone. 'Quite the opposite, in fact.'

Twilight stared at her, puzzled.

'What do you mean?' Lauren asked.

Sidra looked from Lauren to Twilight. 'I, and some of the other Elders, have been watching tonight as you helped the injured girl. It made us realize that although the mirror has chosen Twilight to come back to Arcadia and train as an Elder's assistant, now is not the time. So, Twilight, we have decided that you can stay. It is clear you can do a lot of good with Lauren. As much, maybe even more, than you could do with us in Arcadia.'

'I can stay!' Twilight breathed.

'Will he still have his magic powers?'
Lauren wondered.

Sidra nodded.

'Oh, Twilight!' Lauren gasped, throwing
her arms round his neck.

Sidra smiled. 'You love each other and
deserve to be together. The Unicorn
Elders are sure you will do many good
things.'

'Oh, we will!' Lauren promised. 'At
least we'll try to, won't we, Twilight?'

'Definitely!' he said. 'Thank you! Thank
you so much!'

The unicorn bowed her head again.
'We thank you for all the good deeds you
have already done, and wish you good
luck for the future.' She touched her
magnificent silver horn to Twilight's

forehead and then to Lauren's. Lauren felt
a tingly warm feeling spread through her.

Magic! she thought.

The unicorn blinked warmly at her.
'You are a very special unicorn friend,
Lauren. Very special indeed.'

Lauren felt overwhelmed with pride
and happiness.

'And now I must go,' Sidra said, tossing
back her mane. 'Come, you may fly
beside me some of the way if you wish.'

'Yes, please!' Lauren said and Twilight
nodded eagerly.

Lauren climbed on to his back and
twisted her fingers in his silky mane as he
and the Elder plunged into the sky. The
stars whizzed past in a glittering stream

and the wind whipped Lauren's hair back
from her face. She didn't think she had
ever flown so fast or so high! She laughed
out loud as Twilight tossed his head in
delight and galloped even faster beside
the snow-white Unicorn Elder with the
glittering silver horn.

'I must leave you here!' Sidra said, halting and rearing up against the dark sky. 'Goodbye, Lauren! Goodbye, Twilight! Good luck!'

'Goodbye!' they called.

And with a flash of purple light, Sidra disappeared.

'Oh, wow!' Lauren gasped. 'Wasn't that fun!'

'The best!' Twilight agreed.

'I guess we should go home now,' Lauren sighed. 'Dad will be wondering where I am.'

Circling in the sky, they flew back towards Granger's Farm. They landed at the edge of the woods so Lauren could turn Twilight back to a pony in case her

mum and dad were looking out for
them.

Just before saying the words of the
spell, she pressed her cheek against his
neck. There was one more thing she
wanted to clear up. 'You know that time I
overheard you saying, "I have to tell her"?
You really didn't mean me, did you?'

'No,' Twilight said. 'I was thinking
about Sidra. I knew I had to tell her that
I couldn't leave you.' He turned and blew
gently in her hair. 'I'm sorry you ever
thought I would.'

'I'm sorry too,' Lauren said. 'I should
have trusted you more.'

'And I should have trusted you,'
Twilight replied. 'If I'd told you the truth

from the start, you wouldn't have been so upset.'

'I probably would have,' Lauren admitted, thinking honestly about how she would have reacted if he'd told her he'd been asked to go back to Arcadia. 'But at least we could have talked it through together. Like best friends.' She stroked his nose. 'So from now on, no more secrets. Promise?'

'No more secrets,' Twilight agreed.

Lauren smiled and said the words of the Undoing Spell.

In a flash, Twilight was a pony again. Looking at him standing there, with his fluffy grey coat and pricked-up ears, Lauren felt a rush of love. He was her

pony, her unicorn, but most of all he was
her best friend.

Putting an arm round his neck, she
kissed him. 'Come on,' she said happily.
'Let's go home.'

My Secret Unicorn

When Lauren recites a secret spell, Twilight turns into a beautiful unicorn with magical powers! Together Lauren and Twilight learn how to use their magic to help their friends.

Look out for more My Secret Unicorn adventures:

The Magic Spell,
Dreams Come True, Flying High,
Starlight Surprise, Stronger Than Magic,
A Special Friend, A Winter Wish, A Touch of Magic,
Snowy Dreams, Twilight Magic, Friends Forever, Rising Star,
Moonlight Journey, Keeper of Magic

Do you love magic, unicorns and fairies?

Join the sparkling

My Secret Unicorn

fan club today!

It's FREE!

You will receive
an exciting **online newsletter** 4 times a year,
packed full of fun, games, news and competitions.

How to join:

visit
mysecretunicorn.co.uk
and enter your details

or send your name, address, date of birth* and email address to:

linda.chapman@puffin.co.uk

My Secret Unicorn

Twilight Magic

'Goodness,' said Mrs Wakefield. 'You should feel very honoured, Lauren. Apart from me, you're the only person Apple has approached since Currant's been born. You must have a real way with horses.'

Lauren felt a glow of pride. Jessica and Mel grinned at her but Jade looked cross that Lauren was getting all the attention . . .

My Secret Unicorn
Friends Forever

Lauren looked round to where the other Owls
had been but Jasmine, Natasha, Julia and Rose
had already left to go to the woods. Lauren
wondered if she should catch up with them.
But what would she say? Looking around,
she felt suddenly very alone.

She ran down to the paddocks. Hearing her
coming, Twilight whinnied in greeting and trotted
over to the gate. Lauren put her arms around
him. 'Oh, Twilight,' she whispered . . . 'I never
thought camp was going to be like this!'